Stormy Weather

by

Glen Ebisch

Stormy Weather

Cover Art by *Kristian Norris*

The Wild Rose Press, Inc.
PO Box 708
Adams Basin, NY 14410-0708
Visit us at www.thewildrosepress.com

Publishing History
First Mainstream Mystery Edition, 2017
Print ISBN 978-1-5092-1239-2
Digital ISBN 978-1-5092-1240-8

Published in the United States of America

They both stood on the edge of the hole
staring at something. Reluctantly, I joined them and took a quick glance. The body was face down in the dirt, which, for one crazy moment, made him seem even deader. I caught my breath and glanced away, absorbing what I had seen. A second later, I found my courage and looked back at the body.

"The ground was a little sunken," the small man was saying. "Somebody hadn't tried real hard to put the dirt back. So I knew there must have been some digging here recently. But I never expected to find a body."

"I wouldn't think so," I said.

I found that focusing on the conversation made me calmer. I've always prided myself on being analytical, not giving in easily to my emotions.

"What's that?" the big guy asked. He grabbed a long branch and reached in the hole, turning over a dirty object near the body's head.

"A shame. He was a fan," the man said, as we all recognized the muddy Red Sox logo on the cap.

"Why don't we roll him over and see who he is?" the little guy said, almost jumping up and down with eagerness.

"I think we should wait—" I might as well have been humming Mozart, as the munchkin jumped into the hole to follow his own suggestion.

The body rolled over and stared at the sky.

"Don't know him," the big guy said.

"Neither do I," his friend added.

"I do," I said through clenched teeth, looking into the dead eyes of Travis Lambert.

Praise for Glen Ebisch

Mr. Ebisch has had over twenty-five books, both romances, and mysteries, previously released that have been reviewed in *Publishers Weekly* and *The Kirkus Review* among other publications. His books are usually praised for their humor, thoughtfulness, and vivid characters.

Chapter One

Stormy McCloud…

Of all the things to think about when I can't sleep, I choose to dwell on my name.

I couldn't have picked a better stage name as a television meteorologist. My go-your-own-way mom had given me that moniker. She'd gotten it past my father because he was so disappointed at not having a son that he didn't care what I was called.

It could have been worse—at least that's what I tell myself.

Am I proof that a name is destiny?

Name a girl Sweetness, and she'll be a simpering darling right up until she's booked into the nursing home. I don't believe that any more than I believe every boy named Jesus or Mohammad develops an abiding interest in religion. Names may influence us, but we choose what to make of them.

I was half-considering going back to sleep when I heard a rat-a-tat-tat sound made either by the largest woodpecker in the world or someone at my front door.

I propped myself up on one elbow and looked at the clock through bleary eyes. It read seven-thirty. I always allow myself to sleep to eight-thirty because I work nights, so I rolled over and pretended the sound would go away.

Rat-a-tat-tat!

Annoyed at now being wide-awake, I had to admit to myself that someone was pounding on my front door, and they had no intention of disappearing. Never at my best first thing in the morning, I slowly rolled out of bed. I placed my feet on the floor, then slid them carefully into slippers. On my way past the foot of the bed, I grabbed my robe and pulled it on over my shorts and T-shirt. As I headed down the hall, there was another machine-gun-like rapping. When I got to the door, I peered through the sidelight and saw a trailer with a backhoe parked in my driveway.

What's *this* all about? I shifted my position and saw a large man standing on my front porch. He was tall with a belly that seemed to start in the middle of his chest and extend to his knees, all of it covered in a red knit shirt that threatened to explode at any moment like an overfilled balloon. I opened the door halfway.

"Can I help you?" I asked.

"We're here to dig," he announced as if nothing more needed to be said.

"Dig what?"

"Didn't Bud tell you?"

I assumed he was talking about my landlord, Bud McDonald, but I couldn't bring to mind a mention of digging.

I shook my head.

"We're here to dig the foundation for the garage."

Slowly it came to me, Bud had mentioned, in passing, something about adding a garage to my house. He had brought it up in the context of saying, "If you're going to keep on living here, you'll owe me an extra fifty a month for the garage." But he hadn't been specific about when the construction was to begin, and he certainly hadn't made it sound like it would be within two days of mentioning it.

"Go ahead, then," I said.

"We don't need your permission, we already got the owner's."

"Then why tell me?"

"Just being courteous," he said in a hurt tone.

In the course of our conversation, I had opened the door wider, and he gave me a slow once over, making me aware that my robe stopped well above the knee. When his eyes met mine, he flinched and rocked backward. For a moment, I thought Humpty Dumpty was going to have a great fall, but at the last minute, he regained his balance.

"Anything else?" I asked.

The man shook his head and called to someone in the driveway that he could start unchaining the backhoe. Giving me a final nod, he walked down off the porch.

Deciding that there was no point in trying to go back to sleep with all the noise about to begin outside, I made the bed and quickly got dressed, just in case there was another knock on my front door. In the kitchen, I dumped cereal into a bowl, switched on the television, and started up the coffeemaker.

So now my rent was going to go up. Too bad. I liked my house, a bungalow with mission style touches, such as a stained glass window in the hallway and built-in shelves in the dining area. Aside from those elements, Bud had completely modernized the interior. He never tired of telling me how lucky I was to have the beauty of the old along with the efficiency of the new. I had lived there for about five months and felt like I was just settling in and starting to enjoy the house. But an extra fifty dollars a month could add up, although I had to admit that a garage would be convenient during the long Massachusetts winters.

The throaty roar of a large engine started up outside my kitchen window, sounding like it was in the same room with me. I increased the volume on the small television that sat on my kitchen counter. On the screen Brian Croaker appeared, reporting the weather.

Why is he doing the weather on a Tuesday? Brian was the weekend guy. He was older, semi-retired, and only worked during the week when either Travis Lambert or I, the two regular meteorologists, was out sick. Travis was the morning person. Where was he? He never missed his spot. This past winter he'd had a raging case of the flu and still managed to drag his butt into the studio, looking like a zombie, to do his five-minute broadcast.

Surely Travis hadn't taken a day off. He'd be too afraid his ratings would go down. Popularity was everything to him. As the senior meteorologist by a couple of years, he never let me forget my junior status, frequently warning me that if I kept getting more fan mail than he did, I'd soon find myself looking for another job. I knew he meant it. For Travis, personal vanity justified a world of bad actions. And although I thought sending e-mails to the weatherperson was odd, this was the kind of thing Travis obsessed about. I knew he checked the computer hourly to see whether my website or his was getting more hits. I was also aware that I'd been beating him two to one. I wished it weren't true because having Travis as an enemy wasn't a good thing.

The mere thought of Travis turned the cereal and coffee into sludge in the pit of my stomach. I loved my job but hated the personal conflicts being an on-air personality sometimes led to.

There was another clatter of machine gun fire against my front door. I climbed to my feet and headed down the hall, wondering what further problems the early morning could bring. I opened the door. The big man was on the porch again, staring at me stone-faced.

"There's something you have to see," he said

He turned and got down off the porch. I remained in the doorway, certain there was nothing that this guy could show me so essential to my wellbeing that I had to trot outside before finishing breakfast. The guy must have sensed I wasn't following because his ponderous body swung back to face me.

"You *really* do want to see this."

Reluctantly, I climbed down from the porch and followed as he lumbered around the side of the house. Fortunately, the April morning was fairly warm since all I had on were a sweater and jeans, but I could already feel my sandaled feet getting cold and wet from the heavy dew. A small man sat on top of the backhoe, staring at the ground in front of the machine. He leapt off the equipment and ran toward me.

"You've got to see this," he said, dancing from foot to foot with excitement. That seemed to be the message of the day.

Over the years, I've come to doubt people when they tell me that. I remembered Bobby Miller saying exactly the same thing to me when I was eight, then waggling the largest dead rat I had ever seen in front of my face. Some things stay with you. This guy even reminded me a bit of Bobby, having the same ferrety grin.

I hung back as the two men walked up to the trench they had started to dig not ten feet from my kitchen wall. They both stood on the edge of the hole staring at something. Reluctantly, I joined them and took a quick glance. The body was face down in the dirt, which, for one crazy moment, made him seem even deader. I caught my breath and glanced away, absorbing what I had seen. A second later, I found my courage and looked back at the body.

"The ground was a little sunken," the small man was saying. "Somebody hadn't tried real hard to put the dirt back. So I knew there must have been some digging here recently. But I never expected to find a body."

"I wouldn't think so," I said.

I found that focusing on the conversation made me calmer. I've always prided myself on being analytical, not giving in easily to my emotions.

"What's that?" the big guy asked. He grabbed a long branch and reached in the hole, turning over a dirty object near the body's head.

"A shame. He was a fan," the man said, as we all recognized the muddy Red Sox logo on the cap.

"Why don't we roll him over and see who he is?" the little guy said, almost jumping up and down with eagerness.

"I think we should wait—" I might as well have been humming Mozart, as the munchkin jumped into the hole to follow his own suggestion.

The body rolled over and stared at the sky.

"Don't know him," the big guy said.

"Neither do I," his friend added.

"I do," I said through clenched teeth, looking into the dead eyes of Travis Lambert.

Chapter Two

Hilda Hughes, known around the station as Hildie the Hun for her take-no-prisoners approach to interviewing, shoved the microphone further toward my mouth as though it were a cotton swab and she was demanding a saliva sample. Good luck, nerves had already turned my mouth into something resembling the Sahara. In fact, as I stared across my yard, I began to think that a trip to Timbuktu might be on my short-term agenda. When the News on the Move truck had pulled up in front of my house a few minutes before, I had expected that someone from the station had followed the police scanner and come by to offer sympathy and support. Instead, I had gotten Hildie—vain, ambitious, and thoroughly ruthless Hildie.

"Did you know that Travis' body was residing a mere ten feet from your kitchen?" Hildie asked breathlessly, nodding her head up and down, encouraging me to admit my guilt.

"Of course not," I replied hoarsely. I wasn't even sure dead bodies *resided.* It seemed to me that their residing days were over.

"Do you know who buried Travis' body here?"

"No."

"Do you know why anyone would pick your property to do such a thing?"

I'd had enough. I gave the bulbous end of the

microphone a sharp twist, imagining that I was unscrewing Hildie's little head from her shoulders.

"Ouch!" Hildie said, releasing the microphone into my hands.

"Stop being a jerk."

I gave Sam, the cameraman, the cut sign. Although he had a crush on Hildie that led him to slavishly obey her every whim, even he looked relieved at having an excuse to shut off the camera.

"C'mon, Stormy, this could be my big break," Hildie said in a shrill, wheedling voice.

"Calling me a murderer is going to be your big break?"

"I'm not saying you actually *killed* Travis," Hildie said, and then paused as if giving the idea serious thought. "But you might know who buried the body and be covering up for him or her."

"You think I'm stupid enough to let a killer bury his victim on my front doorstep?"

"Maybe it was only temporary. One of those, sure you can leave him here for a day or two, but he has to be gone by Friday, sorts of things."

"And I had him put the body precisely where my landlord was going to build a garage?"

"You probably forgot about the garage."

She was right on that one. I stayed silent.

"Now how about that interview? Don't worry, I'll try to be balanced and objective," she said in a voice that made me feel like I was biting down on aluminum foil.

An intern last year, while finishing college, Hildie had been hired this year as the station's roving reporter, who got sent out to dig up stuff for the local news segments. It wasn't an easy job, and I had to admit that Hildie was good at getting people to say more than they intended, probably because they wanted more than life itself to be rid of her. She was composed of points: pointy chin, pointy nose, and pointy index finger, which she habitually thrust toward the interviewee's chest as if hoping to reach right in and stimulate a myocardial infarction. Her voice off camera could puncture your eardrums, although on camera she managed to soften it to an almost acceptable sound.

"If you want to interview me, you'll need to get the approval of Simon Harris, and even then I'm not sure I'll talk with you without a lawyer present."

Mentioning the station owner's name stopped Hildie in her tracks. Giving me a disgusted look, as if I were trying to torpedo her one chance at success, she nodded to Sam, who started packing the equipment back in the van. A minute later they drove off, doubtlessly on their way to harass another unfortunate citizen.

I sat on my front steps and tried to use my reason to temper my feeling of concern. I was innocent. So there was no way I could be found guilty of Travis' death, right? But, my analytic mind reminded me, my closest competitor at the station had just been found dead in my yard. No way that looked good. How or why any of this had happened, I had no idea, but everyone would be looking for an explanation, and they would be looking right at me.

I'd already had a taste of this a half-hour earlier. After finding the body, the big guy had pulled a cell phone from the holster on his belt that hung dangerously close to his knees and placed a 9-1-1 call.

The uniformed cop who responded in a few minutes asked some questions starting with "Who lives in this house?" When I admitted that I did, he gave me a long, penetrating look and asked if I knew the victim. I wanted to say that I knew him like a bad rash but confined myself to a nod of the head. When I admitted my knowledge of the deceased, he smiled, clearly confident that this was going to be an easy case to wrap up before lunch by putting me away in the pokey. Next, he asked whether Travis and I were romantically involved. I vehemently denied it and felt so dirty that I wanted to run inside and shower with anti-bacterial soap.

Sensing that things were heading in a bad direction after that interview, I had gone inside and called the television station to talk to Simon Harris, the owner and something of a mentor to me. He had been instrumental in getting me hired and often complimented me on my job performance. When I explained what had happened in a voice that I was pleased to hear remained amazingly calm, like all this was happening to someone else, he told me he would send a person right over to help. I assumed he was referring to a lawyer since I figured I'd soon be in need of legal assistance.

Now, once Hildie had left, I sat on my front porch and waited as more police arrived and a van with what appeared to be forensics people pulled in behind them. No one told me to sit there, but watching everything gave me an illusion of control, as if I could call this whole thing off if it bored me. A short, stocky man who looked like a lawyer and wore a business suit came up the walk and stood in front of me.

"Did Simon Harris send you?" I asked.

He looked confused. "I'm Lieutenant Alan Green. I'm in charge of the detective unit here in the City of Ridley."

I introduced myself although I had a bad feeling that I needed no introduction.

"Do you mind if a couple of my men take a quick look around inside your house?"

My gut told me to say no, and I suspected a lawyer would tell me the same thing. But not wanting to look like I had anything to hide, I agreed.

The Lieutenant nodded to two officers who had come up behind him, and they climbed the stairs and went into my house. Then he took out a spiral notebook and a pen. He remained standing, almost bending over me. He probably meant this to be intimidating, but I just found it annoying. I was tempted to stand up and claim my space but chose to be agreeable for a moment.

"Should I have a lawyer present before answering your questions?" I asked.

"Only if you think you need one. Do you have anything to hide?"

Everyone has something that they want to stay hidden, I thought.

"No," I replied.

"Good. Then it might help us to proceed with our investigation if you could answer at least a few general questions right now."

Wishing my lawyer would hurry up and get here, I reluctantly agreed.

"When did you last see Travis Lambert?"

"At our Friday staff meeting. We get together every Friday afternoon."

"Did you have a conversation with him?"

"Not that I can remember."

"You can't remember if you talked with him?"

I remembered quite well that Travis had given me his usual death ray stare throughout the meeting as if I were a rival gang member encroaching on his turf. But I didn't intend to share that information.

"I may have said hello. Nothing more."

The Lieutenant looked up from his pad.

"What time did you leave the station last night?"

"After the eleven o'clock broadcast. Probably around eleven forty-five."

"Did anyone see you go?"

"I said good night to Maggie Rossiter, the show's producer/director and Ray Johnson, the cameraman."

"Was Travis Lambert there?"

"I doubt it. He's on from six in the morning until two in the afternoon. After that, I take over the weather, and there would be no reason for him to be around."

The Lieutenant carefully wrote in his notebook.

"So from Friday afternoon until today, Tuesday, would it be correct to say that you haven't seen Travis Lambert?"

"Not alive."

The Lieutenant gave me a long look as if checking to see if I was trying to be funny. Not sure, he returned to his questions.

"Did you come home directly from the station last night?"

I nodded.

"Did you notice anyone hanging around your property when you arrived home?"

You mean someone with a shovel and a body? I thought but didn't say. I figured it would label me as a smart aleck and probably a killer.

"I didn't see anyone."

"Was there someone else in the house?"

"It was eleven o'clock at night, and I'm single."

"What about a boyfriend?"

"There was no one else here," I said coolly.

The stone step had become hard, so I stood up and towered over the Lieutenant. Startled, he took a step back.

"We found Travis Lambert's car halfway up the block from your house. Do you know of any reason why he would be in your neighborhood?"

"None at all."

"Was he here to visit you?"

"No. And if he had been, why would he park so far away?"

"Perhaps he was being discreet. Not wanting the neighborhood to know that the two of you were romantically involved. After all, you're both minor celebrities."

The word "minor" hurt, even though it was true.

"We weren't romantically involved," I said, feeling faintly sick at the thought.

"Did you hear anything strange during the night?"

"No."

"Are you a particularly sound sleeper, Ms. McCloud?"

"Why do you ask?"

"It's just hard to believe that you wouldn't have heard someone digging a hole less than ten feet from your house."

"Actually, I am a good sleeper. Plus the blower on the furnace makes so much noise that you couldn't hear the crack of doom in my bedroom."

"And how do you know that the hole wasn't already dug and filled in before Ms. McCloud got home?"

I had been concentrating so much on the Lieutenant that I hadn't noticed someone else had walked across the lawn. Apparently, the Lieutenant hadn't either, because he turned, with annoyed surprise, to face a man, several inches taller than him.

"What are you doing here, Malone? This is an active homicide investigation, not a place for a private investigator."

"The owner of the station, Simon Harris, asked me to look into things to determine if the station has any liability for what happened here. So I'm not, strictly speaking, investigating a homicide."

"Sounds like a subtle distinction to me," Lieutenant Green said.

"So many legal distinctions are," Malone said with a charming smile.

I studied the new arrival, which wasn't too painful. He had light brown hair, blue eyes, and a ruggedly handsome face. He was tall and rather thin, with the kind of body I associate with baseball players. I warned myself not to jump to conclusions, but I disliked him at once, guessing him to be as shallow and conceited as so many attractive men I'd known in the television business. But if Mr. Harris had sent him to help me, I had to at least give him the benefit of the doubt.

He stretched out a hand to me. "I'm Chance Malone."

"Stormy McCloud," I said, taking his hand and happy to meet someone with an equally ridiculous name.

He handed me a card.

"Acme Investigations," I read out loud.

The man raised his hands in a gesture of surrender. "I know. I know. The name is overused and a pathetic attempt to get myself first in the phone book listings. But, what can I say? You have to do what you can to make a living."

"You're not a lawyer?"

Lieutenant Green snorted.

"No, merely a humble private investigator. But Mr. Price, the station lawyer, said I should warn you not to say anything to the police until you've talked to him."

Lieutenant Green gave Malone a smug smile. "That's okay, I've pretty much got everything I need."

I wondered if he meant for a conviction.

He turned to me. "I'll want to talk to you further once we have a preliminary forensics report. And, of course, you may have your lawyer present."

The two officers who had been searching the house came out on the porch. The Lieutenant gave them an inquiring glance. One of the men shook his head, apparently indicating that they had found nothing.

"The door to the basement is locked," the other man said with a meaningful glance as if that was sure to mean something was hidden there.

"Bud MacDonald, my landlord, is the only one with the key to that," I said. "He told me he doesn't want his tenant messing with the mechanicals."

"We'll get a key from MacDonald and check it later," the Lieutenant said.

"But you won't go in the house again without checking with Ms. McCloud or her lawyer, will you?"

Malone said.

"Of course not, unless we have a search warrant," Green replied with a tight smile. Giving me a brief nod, as if promising to see me again soon, he and his men headed around to the back of the house where the police team was working.

Malone watched him walk away.

"He's fair, but I wouldn't want him on my case. Once he gets his teeth into an idea, it's hard to shake him." He glanced at my face. "Sorry, I guess that doesn't make you feel any better."

I took a shot at a casual shrug. "I'm innocent. I don't have anything to worry about."

Chance shook his head. "Don't you watch those newscasts that come on before you do the weather?"

"I always keep up with the news."

"Well, then you must know that the innocent sometimes end up in jail. And as the Bible says, sometimes the evil flourish like a green bay tree."

I bristled at his condescending tone, and I've never liked having the Bible quoted at me.

"I know there's injustice in the world. I'm not a fool."

"Then you should be happy to see me because one of my specialties is keeping the innocent from ending up in jail."

Chance sat down on the top step of the porch and motioned for me to sit next to him. He took out his own little notebook.

"So why don't we begin, Stormy, with you telling me everything you've just told the good lieutenant."

When I was done repeating all the information that I had provided to the police, Malone sat back, with his elbows on the porch behind him, and stared across the street.

"That's not quite everything, is it?"

"What do you mean?"

"I mean you left something out when you talked to the Lieutenant. You didn't mention how you and Lambert didn't get along, am I right?"

"I wouldn't say—"

"There's no point in not telling me the whole truth. After all, I'm on your side."

"How do you know we didn't get along? Did someone at the station tell you?"

Chance shook his head. "I haven't talked to anyone there yet. It's just that I've watched Lambert do the weather a few times, and he's always struck me as a pompous twit. I've watched you do the weather a few times as well, and I can see why a guy like Lambert would feel threatened by you."

I stared at him, sensing that I had just been complimented, but not sure how I felt about praise from this rather infuriating man.

"Okay, I guess that's true," I finally admitted.

"And did he try to get you fired?"

"He threatened to, many times."

"Did you tell any of this to Lieutenant Green?"

I shook my head, and the detective gave me a long look.

"Should I have?" I asked with a sinking feeling.

He shrugged. "Admitting it up front might have made you look more innocent because the police are going to find out all about it once they interview the folks at the station."

"Those people are my friends. They wouldn't say

anything bad about me."

"Maybe not intentionally, but most of them will answer the questions they're asked truthfully, and Lieutenant Green will be sure to ask about how the two of you got along. Plus, there are always a few individuals who *really* want to help the police, and they're happy to volunteer information above and beyond the questions asked. This means that they tend to repeat rumors as if they were certain facts. Mark my words, sooner rather than later, Green will know all about the bad blood between you and Lambert."

"So I should have told him?"

Chance smiled. I had to admit that it was a winning smile, but I suspected he knew all too well the effect it would have on women.

"It's not that important. Of course, it does give you a motive. As for means and opportunity, maybe you heard him prowling around outside your house last night, came out and beaned him with a rock."

"I did no such thing."

"If you did, now is the time to mention it. You could even claim that you thought he was a burglar, didn't recognize him in the dark, and panicked and buried the body once you saw who it was. You might get away with it if you're lucky enough to draw a sympathetic jury."

"I didn't kill him." I paused for a moment. "Is that how he died? Did someone hit him on the head with a rock?"

"I had a brief chat with a friend of mine on the forensics team that's behind your house. Based on the configuration of the wound that's what they're betting on."

"There's a whole rock garden out there along the back of the house. It will be hard to find the right one."

"They can be very persistent, and there should only be one with blood on it."

We sat there side by side for a moment staring across the street, like an old couple watching the world go by. I could barely restrain myself from jumping up and walking around. I felt confined, physically weighed down even, by the evidence piling up against me.

"Have you lived here long?" Chance asked.

"Five months. I moved in last November."

"So you've never seen the yard in bloom. That should be a real treat."

"I'm sure I'll enjoy it if I'm not in prison first."

Chance got to his feet and gave me a boyish smile.

"Don't worry. I'll do my very best to keep that from happening."

I wondered how good his very best was, but didn't say anything.

"I'll be in touch when I come up with something," he said, turning to go. Then he stopped and walked back, standing over me the way Lieutenant Green had. "One last question, why do *you* think Travis Lambert was outside your house when he was murdered?"

"I have no idea."

"That's too bad. Well, think hard about it, because I expect that it's the key to the case."

I stood up on the higher step so I could look into his eyes. Something snapped in me. I was suddenly furious with the way both Green and Malone had treated me. Like I was some little girl who may have dimwittedly committed a crime.

"Look, Mr. Harris hired you, and I have confidence

in him, but your happy-go-lucky attitude doesn't impress me. My general opinion of private detectives is that they make most of their money peering into bedrooms trying to catch married people having affairs. So, I think it's generally a sleazy profession that I'd much prefer to have nothing to do with. The only way I'm going to keep you on the case is if you take me along on every one of your interviews so I can assess the kind of job you're doing. If I don't think you are making a valuable contribution, I'll fire you, whether Mr. Harris agrees or not."

Malone took a step back and grinned.

"Wow! Where did all of that come from? Unless you've had a lot more dealings with private detectives than I think you have, wouldn't you say that you're jumping to conclusions on very little evidence?"

"I've got the evidence of talking to you for the last fifteen minutes, and that hasn't impressed me much. So which is it going to be? Do you take me along or do I give Mr. Harris a thanks-but-no-thanks call?"

Malone's face became thoughtful. "I've never worked with a partner before, especially not a partner who was a client."

"I have a logical mind, and I know these people. I can be helpful to you."

"I guess I could make an exception this time." He paused. "I'll do it as a favor to you."

"A favor?"

"Because you really need me; you just don't know how much yet."

Chapter Three

As soon as I got in the house, I sat on the bed and hugged myself as tightly as I could. At no time had I ever been more afraid. Part of my outburst at Malone had been fear in another form. By shouting at him, I was doing something, instead of watching passively while the case against me grew. I needed to talk to someone who would take my situation seriously but be calm and rational enough to give me good advice. The only person I could think of that filled the bill was my father. We didn't always get along, but I relied on him for his clear insights.

I checked my watch. My father would be teaching at the college today, but he had an office hour right about now. I picked up my cell phone and punched in his number. When I heard his deep, rich voice answer, my heart rate slowed.

"Hi, Dad, it's me."

"What's wrong, Stormy?"

"Why should anything be wrong?" I asked, annoyed that he seemed to already know the situation.

"First of all, you never call me at work unless something serious has come up, and secondly, I can tell that something is wrong by the artificially happy tone of your voice."

I sighed and poured out the whole story. I tried to do it in an orderly, concise way that would appeal to the mind of a mathematician. When I was done, I waited without speaking, knowing my father was, as usual, taking time to frame his response.

"So as I understand it, you are a suspect because this man's body was found on your property, and as will soon come out, you didn't get along well in the workplace."

"Precisely."

"And you have no idea how he came to be buried in your yard?"

"None at all." I was getting tired of that question.

Again there was a long pause.

"I think the first thing you need to show is that there were other people who might have wished to harm this man. From what you've told me about him, he sounds like a person who would have made a number of enemies. You need to demonstrate that one of these people may have killed him and is trying to point the finger of blame at you."

"But that implies planning. If you planned something out, you wouldn't rely on finding a rock that you could use as a weapon," I said.

"Good point."

I felt myself preen as I always did when I earned my father's praise.

"However, it's possible that the killer scoped out your property beforehand and removed a rock to be used later as a weapon."

"I suppose," I said, disappointed that he had found a way around my objection so easily.

"Right now there's no point in speculating. We don't have enough information. I think you should do as you planned and stay in close contact with this private investigator and make sure he does his job. Don't let your personal dislike of him blind you to seeing him as a valuable ally. You should also have a conversation with the station's lawyer to see if you should retain legal counsel."

My stomach tightened at the word *legal.*

"Do you think it will come to that?"

"I hope not, Stormy, and I think it's too soon to jump to that conclusion, but you should have a good lawyer present the next time you are questioned by the police."

"Yes, I suppose you're right. I was afraid that getting a lawyer would make me look guilty."

"Getting a lawyer will make you look smart. And that's what you have to be when confronting a situation like this."

I tried to corral my emotions and keep my rational mind in the forefront.

"Is there anything else that I need to do?"

"I don't believe so." My father hesitated for a moment. "Would you like me to come there to be with you? I can leave right now."

Dad taught at Jamesburg College in the northern Berkshires, and he could be in Ridley in about an hour and a half.

I knew how much of a sacrifice it was for him to volunteer to leave in the middle of a class day. The only classes my father had missed in over thirty years of teaching were on the day my mother left us. That was back when I was seven, and she ran off with another man. My father took his responsibilities seriously and expected others to do likewise.

"I don't think that will be necessary right now," I

said, at the same time thinking how nice it would be to have my father sitting next to me.

"Very well," he said.

I could tell by the relief in his voice that I had made the right decision.

"Well, I appreciate the good advice, and I'll act on it."

"Have you considered that none of this would have happened if you were in another line of work?"

I stifled a sigh. He always knew how to ruin it. Just when I was thinking how great he was, he had to bring up the old argument that I should have gone into science or mathematics and become an academic like himself. I couldn't believe he was going to raise this old point of contention right now when I had so many other problems.

"People get murdered on college campuses, too."

"Of course, but being around as many large egos as there are in the entertainment industry is bound to increase the crimes of passion. People killing others because they have more fame, fortune, or adulation. A television station must be a hotbed for such things."

"I don't think it's quite as bad as you think," I said. Before he could expand on the theme, I quickly went on. "I'll be in touch with you in a few days to let you know how things are going."

"Very well. And, Stormy, good luck."

For my father to resort to luck was a sign of how concerned he really was.

Chapter Four

At one o'clock, I pulled into the parking lot next to the low white building that housed WAQB. It was next to a transmitter tower on top of Devin Mountain just within the boundaries of Ridley, a small city in western Massachusetts. Malone and I had agreed to meet there to begin our joint investigation. The police had said I could lead my normal life as long as I didn't leave the area without notifying Lieutenant Green. I sat in the car waiting for the song on the radio to end and thought about Malone.

Once he got over his initial reluctance, he had seemed to adjust pretty well to the idea of having me join him in the investigation, but I was still going to have to keep an eye on him. He was a smooth operator, and I wouldn't put it past him to say one thing and do another. I saw his car pull into the lot. I waited a second then got out and walked over to meet him.

"You're a couple of minutes late," I said.

He checked his watch and smiled. "Not according to my time."

I decided not to argue and led him in the direction of the front door.

"Where do you want to start?" I asked.

"Eventually I hope to talk to everyone. But why don't you choose where to begin."

I paused to think. "Why don't we start right at the

front door and work our way back?"

"Fine. Just one thing, let me take the lead in asking the questions. If I miss anything, you can always step in at the end. Okay?"

I nodded but mentally reserved the right to butt in whenever I thought it necessary.

Malone held open the double glass doors, and we went down the short hall to where the attractive young woman who worked as the receptionist looked up with an eager smile. Her smile turned into an expression of surprise when she saw me like she didn't expect an almost accused murderer to show up for work.

"This is Mia Berkeley," I said to Malone.

"Hi, I'm Chance Malone. I'm a private investigator working for Mr. Harris on the Lambert case," he said, giving her a charming smile and shaking her eagerly extended hand. He opened a wallet with his credentials and held it out in front of her. Mia barely glanced at it.

"Are you a real private eye?" she asked, melting before our eyes.

"About as real as they come, licensed and everything."

Her face took on an expression of awe.

"Are you the receptionist?" he asked.

"Technically I'm an administrative assistant. That means I answer the phone and do whatever gofer work needs doing. I pretty much run the front office."

"Did you know Mr. Lambert well?"

"Poor Travis," Mia said, struggling to put a sad expression on her face. I wondered what she had against him. "I didn't know Travis really well, but this is a small place, so you get to know everyone a little bit."

"You knew him well enough not to care for him, though. Am I right?" Malone said.

I guessed he had spotted her equivocal expression just as I had.

Her jaw dropped slightly as if she had witnessed a magic act.

"How did you know that?"

"Aside from his being pompous and a bit full of himself, why else didn't you like him?"

Mia blushed and shot a glance down the empty hall. Then she leaned across the counter and dropped her voice to a stage whisper.

"He wanted to go out with me. I told him he was way too old. I'm only twenty-two, and he had to be over thirty."

"How did he respond to your refusal?" Malone asked.

"He pretty much told me that if I didn't date him, he'd get me fired."

"That's terrible," I said. "You should have filed a complaint against him with management."

Malone gave me an annoyed look. I figured that I'd stepped in early. Too bad, it was my neck on the line.

"I've only been here two months," Mia said. "Who do you think management is going to believe if he made up some story about me? He gave me until next week to decide. I've been half sick trying to figure out what to do."

Malone nodded his head in sympathy. "Did you tell anyone here about what he was up to?"

"I told Ray, one of the cameramen. He said I should talk to Mrs. Hayes. She's the station manager."

"Did you do that?"

Mia shook her head, making her shoulder-length blonde hair swirl. "I was working up my courage. I wasn't sure she would believe me. Plus I didn't want to start trouble unless I absolutely had to."

Malone saw me about to speak and shook his head slightly. Reluctantly, I kept my mouth shut.

"That's completely understandable," he said.

She nodded. "I took the job here because eventually, I want an on-air position. I majored in communications in college, so I don't want to be a glorified receptionist my whole life. But if I complained about the senior weatherman, I figured my career would be over before it starts."

"I get your point," Malone said. "Now just to make sure I have my facts straight, where were you last night?"

Her eyes went wide. "Am I a suspect? I didn't do anything to Travis."

"I'm sure you didn't," Malone said soothingly. "But I have to be able to say in my report where everyone was at the time of the murder. It's also a way to eliminate suspects. You understand, right?"

"Sure, I suppose. I live with my parents. I don't make enough here to afford my own place yet."

"Were you at your parents' the whole night? And were they home?"

"They were there," she rolled her eyes, "and I didn't go out at all."

"Well, then, I guess that lets you off the hook," Chance said with a smile that suggested he couldn't be happier.

Mia smiled back. "You seem awfully nice for a private detective. I thought they were these tough guys who tried to frighten people into confessing."

Chance leaned over the counter and dropped his voice. "What I would like to know is whether you can think of anyone else who might have had a disagreement with Mr. Lambert?"

Mia fidgeted and cast a sidelong glance in my direction.

"Don't be afraid to tell the truth," Malone said. "Ms. McCloud will understand."

I wasn't so sure about that.

"Well, I don't think Stormy and Travis got along. Of course, everybody knew that, so I'm not saying anything to get her into trouble," the girl said, giving me a nervous smile. "But she couldn't have killed him."

"Why not?" Malone asked. I wanted to hear the answer to that one myself.

"Stormy is too smart to murder someone and then bury the body in her own yard. If she killed someone, the body would be long gone by now."

Malone suppressed a smile while Mia looked at me proudly as if she had just proven herself a true friend. I didn't think the "too-smart-to-kill defense" was going to fly with Lieutenant Green.

"Is there anyone else who had a problem with Travis?" Malone asked.

"Do you know Holland Finch?" Mia whispered.

"I've seen him on television."

"He's the senior anchor on the evening news. Well, Holly and Travis had a big fight yesterday around noon. Holly came in early and caught Travis as he was leaving. I think Holly planned it that way. He was furious and wanted to have it out with Travis."

"Do you know what it was all about?"

"Not really. But I heard that it had something to do with Holly's daughter, Kelly."

"Did Travis know Holly's daughter?"

"She works here as an intern. She's still in high school."

"Do you think Travis tried the same thing with her that he did with you?"

Mia smiled smugly and shook her head. "Kelly is this pathetically skinny little thing with absolutely no personality as all. She mopes around all the time and hardly does any work. I'm sure they keep her on just because of her father."

"But you don't know the specific cause of the fight."

"Nope. All I know is that Holly got the worst of it."

Malone took a step back from the counter and glanced at me in case there was anything I wanted to ask. I shook my head.

"Is there anything else about Travis that you can tell me?"

"Well, just yesterday Hildie Hughes, you know, the one who does the reports from the field?"

Malone nodded.

"She was saying that she'd happened to see Travis and Debbie Cummings, the junior nighttime anchorperson, having dinner on Saturday night at a romantic little place over in Springfield. No one suspected that the two of them had hooked up. It spread all around the station yesterday. I figured that maybe it would take me off of Travis's radar. If he had Debbie, maybe he'd leave me alone."

"I guess it doesn't matter now that he's dead," Malone said.

She thought for a moment then brightened. "No, I guess not."

Malone smiled and pointed down the hall. "Would it be all right if I spoke to the other folks who work here?"

Of course, it would be all right, I wanted to say, but Malone gave me a stifling look.

"Since Mr. Harris hired you, I'm sure it would be okay," Mia replied.

She pointed to a gate at the end of the counter.

"Go right through there and down the hall. Along the hall are the offices of the owner, the manager, and the marketing people. At the end of the hall is the bull pen, a big open space with desks for all the junior people."

"Where would I find Holly Finch?"

"There are six glassed-in cubicles around the outer edge of the bull-pen. One of them is Holly's." She checked the watch on her wrist. "It's three o'clock. He should be in by now getting his material ready for the five-thirty newscast."

Chance thanked Mia and followed her directions.

"I could have told you how to get to the offices," I hissed in his ear.

"I wanted to treat Mia with respect. She seems like a good source of information."

"You mean by suggesting that I'm too smart to have murdered Travis?"

Malone smiled. "At least she wasn't accusing you."

"But she had a good reason herself to want Travis dead. When Green finds out about that, it should take some of the pressure off of me."

"She had motive, but not the opportunity. She was

home with her parents."

"According to her."

"I'll check it out with her parents."

"Who would no doubt lie to protect her."

Malone shrugged. "We'll see."

"Well, you were right about one thing," I said.

"About what?"

"You said that someone would volunteer that Travis and I didn't get along, and that's what Mia did right out of the gate."

Malone shrugged. "I've been doing this for a while, and people are pretty predictable." He gave me an amused glance. "Does this mean that you're satisfied with the way I'm doing my job?"

"The jury's still out," I replied. Instantly regretting my choice of words.

Chapter Five

I trailed along as Chance followed Mia's directions. I glanced over and saw that my desk, which was set along the wall away from the others, was empty. I figured Brian had left for the day after I had called in and told them I'd be showing up a little late for my shift. Four of the six glass cubicles were empty. Debbie Cummings, an attractive blonde who for some mysterious reason apparently had a thing for Travis, occupied one of the remaining two. In the other cubicle was a middle-aged man with an impressive head of gray hair. This was Holland Finch, the senior newsman at the station. I pointed him out to Chance.

"Since he had a fight with Travis, let's talk to him next," Chance said.

I nodded.

We took up a position at the entrance to the cubicle, but Finch didn't notice. He was staring into a hand-held mirror doing what appeared to be neck-tightening exercises. They seemed to involve sticking his chin out as if daring someone to take a poke at it, then suddenly pulling his head in like a turtle. I noticed that he had a serious-looking bruise on his right temple. After a few seconds, he switched over to an exercise that involved pulling his face into the shape of a tightly closed fist, then suddenly expanding it into an exaggerated expression of surprise. While doing this, he caught sight of Malone, and his surprise became genuine.

"Who are you?" he growled in his finest anchorman's voice.

Malone stepped into the cubicle and stuck out his hand.

"Chance Malone, private investigator. I've been hired by Mr. Harris to look into the Travis Lambert case."

Finch briefly shook the offered hand. He looked at me, but beyond a nod, didn't react.

Since the only visitor's chair in the office was covered with a pile of papers, Chance leaned casually against the wall, while I stayed in the doorway.

"Can you tell me what you know about Travis Lambert?"

"I didn't know Lambert all that well. He worked days, and I work nights. I was certainly surprised to hear that his body turned up on Ms. McCloud's property. I'm sure she had nothing to do with his death."

I gave him a quick smile of appreciation.

Malone took a step away from the wall toward Finch and stared hard at him.

"I heard you had an altercation with Mr. Lambert yesterday afternoon. What was that about?"

"That was personal," Finch replied, practicing his closed-fist face.

"I'm sure it was. But Mr. Harris wants this story to go away as soon as possible, and the only way that's going to happen is if we let in a little sunlight and find out the truth. That means that the personal has now become the public."

Holly Finch sighed. "It had to do with my daughter."

"That would be Kelly, who works here as an intern?"

"So you've been asking around already."

"Guilty as charged," Malone replied amiably.

"Heck of a job, poking your nose into other people's business," Finch said.

"It has its compensations."

Finch grunted his doubts. "Kelly has had a problem with drugs for quite some time now. Her mother and I have put her in rehab repeatedly, but it never seems to take. I thought that getting her a job here would help develop her sense of responsibility. All the experts say that increasing an addict's sense of self-worth is the first step in ending her addiction."

"So what happened?"

"Having this job was helping Kelly, or so I thought," Holly said. He frowned as if wondering whether he had only been deluding himself. "But I could tell that Kelly was high on something on Friday night. I've gotten so that I can recognize the signs. Over the weekend I forced her to tell me where she had gotten the drugs from, and it turned out that Travis had given her cocaine. That's why I confronted Lambert in the parking lot yesterday. I asked him what he thought he was doing giving drugs to an underage addict. The bastard just laughed and said that she had to make up her own mind about what she would and would not do. He even suggested that she'd be better off if we let her lead her own life."

"What did you say to that?"

"I threatened to tell Mr. Harris that he was giving

drugs to a minor. He told me to go ahead that I had no proof aside from the word of my addicted daughter. He also promised me that if I did tell Harris, the court would find out that Kelly had used drugs. As part of her suspended sentence, she can't be caught using. I knew Travis would be as good as his word, and I couldn't have Kelly thrown into some juvenile facility."

"Is that when you hit him?"

Finch smiled ruefully and fingered the bruise on his forehead. "I *tried* to hit him, but he was years younger and in a lot better shape. He knocked me down, then got in his car, and drove away."

"What did you do after that?"

"I came back inside." Finch nodded to the cubicle next to his where Debbie Cummings was looking over some papers. "Debbie, my co-anchor, put a cold compress on my head and managed to convince me not to go running to Harris with a complaint. Now that I've had some time to think about it, I realize she was right. Even if I got Lambert fired, which isn't a sure thing the way companies coddle drug users today, it would have been bad for Kelly."

"But you were here last night, so you stayed to do your evening show," I interrupted.

Why had no one told me yesterday about the fight between Travis and Holly? But I'm not one for spreading stories, so I get left out of the loop a lot. There's a certain reciprocity to gossip.

Finch shrugged. "Of course, the bruise was easy to cover up with makeup."

"How long were you here at work?" asked Malone.

"I was on air at five-thirty, six, and then I did the eleven o'clock."

"What did you do after that?"

"I went directly home. My wife and I planned to have a long talk with Kelly."

"Did you see Lambert again after the altercation in the parking lot?"

"No."

"You didn't go looking for him to get even?"

"And take another beating?"

"Maybe, this time, you took something along to even things up."

He shook his head. "I may have been angry enough to kill when I took that swing at him, but by the end of the night, I'd cooled down and thought things through. I realized that the problem was with Kelly, not Lambert. There are always people around who are going to be willing to sell or even give her drugs, and she has to be strong enough to deal with that if she's going to beat this thing. I can't protect her from everyone who will try to lead her astray."

Malone thanked Finch for his time, and we left the cubicle. I was about to ask Malone where he wanted to go next, when a throaty voice said, "Excuse me." Debbie Cummings stood next to us, fidgeting nervously.

Malone put on another one of his charming smiles.

"What can I do for you?"

"Can we go somewhere to talk for a moment…in private?"

From the way she looked at me, I figured I wasn't to be included in this little chat.

"I'm sorry," Malone said, "but Ms. McCloud has to be part of any conversations I have here."

"Oh, all right," Debbie said, with a little pout.

"Follow me."

She led us back up the hallway to the front desk and opened the door to an office marked *Marketing*.

"The marketing people don't come in on Tuesdays, so we can talk in here."

We sat down around a small conference table.

"You're Debbie Cummings, the anchorperson. Am I right?" Malone let enough awe seep into his voice that I wanted to hit him.

She nodded.

"I watch you and Holly Finch all the time."

Debbie smiled and ran her fingers through her blonde hair, her self-confidence returning at the prospect of dealing with a fan.

"Did you want to talk to me about the Travis Lambert case?" he asked.

"I overheard what Holly told you. Those glass walls aren't really soundproof." She paused and took a deep breath. "I just don't want you to get the wrong idea about Travis. He really wasn't the monster that some people make him out to be."

"So he didn't give Kelly Finch drugs?" Malone said.

"Well, I suppose he did, but you have to know Kelly. She heard a rumor that Travis sometimes used drugs, so she was always around him begging for the stuff. Holly doesn't realize how persistent she can be. I think it was a combination of feeling sorry for her and just wanting to get rid of her that made Travis give her something. And it's not like he asked her for money or anything."

How long would it have been before he started making her pay? I was having trouble picturing Travis as a drug-dealing humanitarian.

"It was nice of you to help Holly after his fight with Travis," Malone said.

"Holly was so angry I thought he'd get Travis fired. I managed to calm him down while I was putting the compresses on his head."

"It seems like you took quite an interest in Travis' well being."

Debbie blushed slightly in a way that men probably found charming. I thought it made her appear juvenile.

"Travis and I had sort of a thing going."

"Then I'm sorry for your loss," Malone said.

She nodded, and her eyes filled with tears. "We didn't go out for very long. I've worked here for a little over three months, and we've only been together for about six weeks. But once we got started, it was like a house on fire, and I think it was heading in the direction of becoming something serious." Debbie bent forward and pulled a gold necklace with a jeweled heart pendant from inside her neckline. "Travis gave me this just last week."

I glanced at the necklace. It looked like the sort of thing Travis would have bought by the bushel.

"Very nice," Malone said. "I gather Travis wanted to keep your relationship a secret?"

"He was just trying to look out for my best interests. He said Mr. Harris wasn't a believer in office romances, and I might get fired."

He had a secret affair with Debbie while he tried to blackmail Mia into going out with him. The guy was amazing. I had never liked Travis, but not being tuned into the station grapevine, I'd never realized what good reasons I had for feeling that way. Clearly, Travis was a devious, self-serving bum, especially good at manipulating women.

Debbie gave Malone a smile that was both helpless and flirtatious. I wished I could manage an expression like that without being ironic.

"Will you have to tell anyone in authority about my relationship with Travis? I know it's gotten around the station since Hildie saw us, but I'm not sure it's reached management. I really need my job here."

"I can't promise you anything. If it's relevant to solving the case, it will have to become known. And I would strongly recommend that you tell the police about it when they come to question you."

"The police are going to question me?" she asked, her eyes growing wide with alarm.

"I'm sure they're going to question everyone here. Don't be nervous. Just tell them the truth," Malone advised, putting a soothing hand on her shoulder. We stood. He opened the door and escorted Debbie out into the hall. Still looking worried, she headed back to her cubicle.

Chapter Six

"I have to go to work now," I said. "That means our investigating is over for the day."

"Will you give me permission to call Mia's parents and Holly's wife to check on their alibis?" Chance asked.

I paused for a moment. "I guess that will be all right."

"When will you be free again?"

I checked my watch. "At two-fifteen, but I can't leave the studio. I have to start studying the computer models for tomorrow."

"But you can give me a few more minutes then?"

"Sure."

Flashing me another one of his charming smiles, he turned and headed up the hall to the exit.

Twenty minutes later, I glanced at the clock on the wall over my desk and saw that it was time for me to get ready for the mid-afternoon weather update. That's a fifteen second spot where I cover the weather for the next few hours and give a quick preview of the evening report. I pulled the one graphic I needed off the computer and fed it into the studio computer where Maggie Rossiter, my producer/director, would see that it appeared on the wall behind me at the click of a remote. I then typed into the computer what I was going to say and sent that out as well. I still had five minutes before I had to walk across the hall to the studio, and my mind wandered to Chance Malone.

He was certainly an attractive man. Even his offbeat sense of humor might be appealing to me if I weren't so uptight right now about Travis' death. But I'd known men like that before. My father had told me that it was a man with a *way with words* who had stolen my mother from him with extravagant promises and impossible dreams. Their relationship hadn't lasted long, but my father had refused to take her back. She had stayed in California and never remarried. I had only seen her infrequently when I was young, the last time being on my twelfth birthday. I remembered her as a sad woman filled with regrets.

I checked the clock again and realized I was late. I rushed across the hall to the studio.

"I was about to send the bloodhounds out for you," Maggie said as the big soundproof door closed behind me.

"Sorry, I had a couple of things on my mind."

Maggie looked stricken. "Of course you did. That was really insensitive of me. It's amazing you even came into work today. You're a real trouper." She came over and gave me a hug. Over her shoulder, I saw Ray, the cameraman.

"Bad scene about Travis," he mumbled, giving me a sympathetic nod. "Not that the guy couldn't be a pain about camera angles sometimes. But I guess I shouldn't say bad things about the dead."

"I'm more worried about people saying bad things about me, like that I'm a killer."

Maggie drew back in surprise. "A killer? Who would think that?"

"The police, for one. I think I'm pretty high on their suspect list."

"Cops!" Ray said in disgust. "They'll blame anybody just to get a case off the books."

Dressed in a torn T-shirt and ragged jeans that revealed several tattoos, Ray always looked like he might have direct knowledge of the penal system. But in my experience, the behind-the-camera people always seemed to make a point of appearing extremely casual, so Ray's attire probably didn't mean anything.

Maggie pushed her oversized retro glasses higher up on her nose.

"Why do they suspect you?"

"Because the body was found on my property. You have to admit that is kind of suspicious."

Maggie paused for a moment. "I guess somebody might see it that way, come to think of it. Do you have any idea why Travis was out at your house in the middle of the night?"

I shook my head.

"The two of you weren't going together?"

"Not a chance. We didn't even like each other."

"It's almost air time," Ray announced, getting behind the camera.

Maggie stood right in front of me and stared at my face as if it were a problem to be solved.

"A little powder will do it for today."

She quickly picked up a small disposable powder puff from her table and pressed some makeup onto my nose and upper forehead. We spent ten seconds running through the visuals then we were on the air. I did my fifteen seconds. As soon as we were off, Ray headed down the hall to the break room, no doubt needing coffee to restore his strength.

"Have you heard anything from Mr. Harris about whether you'll be getting promoted to head meteorologist?" Maggie asked.

"I haven't even thought about it. Right now I'm more concerned with whether I'll end up in jail."

"That's not going to happen," Maggie said firmly. "Now I know you've been here less than six months, but you've done a fine job. And you're a whole lot easier to work with than most of our other on-air personalities."

"You mean like Holly, complaining that Ray comes in for his close up at the wrong time just to make him look bad."

I smiled to myself at how we were like a large family, where each person had to adjust to the other's eccentricities. I also realized how much I would miss all this if it were taken away from me.

Maggie nodded. "Not that Ray can't be a real pill once in a while himself, but he's a professional behind the camera. Holly is just too sensitive. Anyway, if the powers that be ask my opinion, I'm going to suggest that they give you Travis' job and find somebody to replace you."

"It seems too ghoulish to even talk about right now, but thanks, Maggie."

We hugged again.

"Orthoclase feldspar," Maggie whispered in my ear.

I began to laugh.

Orthoclase feldspar was the only term I remembered from my semester of geology, and since Maggie was a rock collector—a real rock hound—we had developed this little inside joke that meant good luck.

Maggie squinted at me in her motherly way. "Are you sure you'll be okay?"

I nodded. "Don't worry, I'll be fine."

I returned across the hall to my desk and began focusing on the evening weather forecast. Since sunny and seasonable weather was expected to continue for the next two days, I began looking out over the rest of the week for something more interesting. Although I didn't like the unsettled, stormy weather of winter because it brought so much hardship to people, long spells of nice weather can be pretty boring from the forecasting perspective. I was concentrating so much that I hardly noticed when Malone slipped into the chair next to my desk.

"I come bearing information, but I'm afraid it's not helpful."

"Let's hear it."

"Mia's mother swears that her daughter was in the house from seven o'clock until the next morning."

"She could have slipped out with no one hearing her."

"Possible, but not likely. I got the distinct impression her parents watch her like hawks. Holly's wife says that he was home by quarter to twelve on Monday night. And they spent the next three hours having some kind of intervention with Kelly."

"She could be lying, too."

Malone shrugged.

"What about Debbie? Maybe she found out about Travis and Mia and killed him for the philandering fool he was."

Malone gave another of his infuriating shrugs.

"The problem is that his body was found in your yard."

"Thanks for pointing that out."

"Can you think of any reason why Holly, Mia, or Debbie would want to implicate you in a murder?"

"No, and none of them has ever been to my house. They probably don't even know where I live."

"I'm sure the station keeps a list of addresses somewhere. I'll check and find out if it's easily accessible to the people who work here." Malone looked at the wall behind him. "I see you have the only window. Is that so you can look outside if the computer goes on the fritz?"

"Believe it or not, I've heard that one before," I said.

The computer on my desk gave a beep, and the screen filled with data.

"Do you get a break or do they expect you to keep your nose to the computer all day?"

"Weather changes so quickly in New England, you've got to stay on top of it. Otherwise, your forecast is yesterday's news."

Malone pretended to be stunned for a moment. "Was that an instance of humor, Stormy?"

"I can be very funny when I'm not involved in a murder case."

"Yes, that does tend to put a damper on things." Malone glanced around. "I was serious. Is there a place to take a break around here? I could use something to drink."

"This way," I said and led him down a side hallway into a room with greenish linoleum floors and white walls in desperate need of a coat of paint. Four tables with plastic chairs around them filled up the center of the floor, but no one was there. A half-full coffeepot simmered on the burner next to a partially eaten cake. In the corner were a soda and a snack machine.

"I've had my quota of coffee for today," Malone said, approaching the soda machine.

"If you tip the machine forward, you can get a free bottle about half the time."

Malone nodded but took some change out of his pocket.

"I'd rather pay. Small evils lead to bigger ones. Plus this way I get to choose my flavor."

He returned to the table with an orange soda, an odd choice for a tough-guy detective.

"So did you want to interrogate me further?" I asked. "Fire away, but I'm afraid I've already told you everything I know."

Malone took a long drink of soda. "How did you come to be a weather person?"

I raised an eyebrow.

"Is that necessary for you to know?"

"Humor me."

"That's part of a long story about my search for a major in college and how I happened to enroll in a course in meteorology and loved it. Being a student who learned math and science easily, I decided to make it a career."

"Where did you go to college?"

"Jamesburg."

Chance's eyebrows slid up. "Pretty high quality place."

"My father works there."

"I see."

"No, you don't. I didn't get in because of my father. I had almost all A's in high school and just about perfect SATs."

He grinned. "Okay. Now I see. You're a smart lady."

"And don't forget it."

"Meteorology sounds like a challenging field of study."

"It is, and today the degree is essential. There was a time when weather people on television didn't need any background in meteorology. They were, just in the case of women at least, pretty faces reading off cue cards. Today you need a degree to get the job, and it helps to be certified by the American Meteorological Society.

"But it still helps to be a pretty face."

I felt my cheeks get warm. "It doesn't hurt."

"How did you end up on television? Was that something you planned?"

I shook my head. "In my senior year, I heard about an internship with a local television station. I hadn't given any real thought to what I was going to do with my major, so I gave it a try. I found that I liked being at the station. At first, I spent most of my time just shadowing the weather people, but finally, they let me work up a demo. No one was surprised as much as me when I got a job offer from a small station out in Pennsylvania. I was there four years, then I moved here last fall."

Chance seemed focused on making rings with his soda can on the tabletop. I couldn't tell how carefully he was listening to the recital of my past. I found myself staring at his sinewy arm turning the can around and around.

"Why did you move to western Mass? Is it a bigger market?"

I hesitated for a moment. "A little bigger, plus, of course, I originally came from around here."

"Your parents must be very proud when they see you on television."

"My mother lives far away, and my father doesn't watch."

"Why not?"

"He wanted me to go into college teaching like himself. He thinks I'm wasting my talent."

"Parents can be difficult. My mother still asks me when I'm going to become a lawyer."

I smiled. "But my life was pretty good up until now."

"And then you ran into Travis Lambert, a real obstacle in your career path."

"Nothing I wouldn't have worked around over time."

"Still, a problem for you."

"But I didn't want to see him dead."

"Even if you had, that would have put your name on a rather long list. After all, he was blackmailing Mia, giving drugs to Kelly, and probably planning to cheat on Debbie."

"What kind of monster was he?" I asked.

"Pretty small by criminal standards, but typical of the kind of low life that manages to thrive in the nooks and crannies of respectable businesses. He gets away with it because most people are decent and don't want trouble."

"Do you really think Mia, Debbie, or Holly killed him, then?" I whispered.

Malone shook his head. "Even leaving aside their alibis, it doesn't make sense. It seems to me that Mia would have complained to her boss before committing murder. Holly would be a fool to murder someone he had publicly attacked only a few hours before. And, as far as we know, Debbie didn't know Travis was planning to cheat on her."

"So I'm still suspect number one."

"Patience, Stormy, we're just getting started."

I sat back and studied Malone. He had the loose-limbed, relaxed look of an athlete. He was lean but had the muscled shoulders and arms of someone who worked-out. He gave me one of his big boyish smiles as if he were an open book.

"Since you asked me how I chose my career, how did you come to choose yours? Not many people become private detectives."

The smile disappeared from his face. He quickly gulped down the last of his soda, crushed the can, and neatly tossed it into the garbage barrel in the corner of the room. He got to his feet.

"Right now you're part of an ongoing investigation. Maybe some time after this case is solved we can get together and discuss my life."

I watched him walk out of the room. I had clearly hit a sore spot. I was surprised how much his unwillingness to answer made me want to know more about the man.

Chapter Seven

I had just returned to my desk and started to organize my evening broadcast when my phone rang. It was Simon Harris, the station owner, and he wanted me to come to a meeting in his office right away. In the short walk to the meeting, my mind raced through half a dozen possible reasons why he might want to speak to me, ranging from my immediate firing to my promotion into Travis' slot.

I knocked on the door and was told to come in. Mr. Harris, a distinguished looking man in his late sixties, was sitting behind the desk. On a chair in front of him sat Clarissa Hayes, the station manager, an attractive woman in her forties. There was also a short gray haired man who was introduced as Harvey Price, the station's lawyer. The other person in the room was Chance Malone, looking slightly embarrassed at seeing me so soon after his dramatic exit.

I had always considered Harris a surrogate father, warmer and more understanding than my real one. The fact that he currently looked so worried made me extremely uneasy.

"Nice to see you, Stormy," Mr. Harris said, reaching across the desk to shake my hand. "We wanted to know how Mr. Malone's investigation is coming along, and he said that he'd promised you'd be privy to everything that went on. So here you are."

I nodded my thanks to Malone, who smiled slightly.

When I was seated, Mr. Harris began. "Clarissa and I were talking about how to go about replacing Travis. We have a part-timer, Brian Croaker, who can fill in temporarily, but we really have to start looking for a new weather person right away. Even if you move up into Travis' slot, someone will have to replace you."

I relaxed a bit. I liked the way the conversation was going so far.

"How did you come to employ Travis in the first place?" asked Malone.

Harris looked over at Clarissa. "He came with high recommendations from a station out near Troy, New York," she answered. "His demo was good, and he seemed very professional. We had him on probation for a couple of months then gave him a contract. He was pretty popular with the viewers."

"How long had he worked here?"

"About two years."

"Ever have any complaints about him?"

Clarissa frowned. "What sort of complaints? If you meant complaints from viewers, there are always a few of them whenever the weather person gets something wrong. Blaming the messenger for the message, that sort of thing."

"I was thinking more of complaints from his colleagues."

"Not complaints as such. I would sometimes overhear comments from people that suggested they didn't particularly care for him. I can't say I was surprised because I didn't like him much myself."

Malone's eyebrows went up. "Why was that?"

"He had an attitude that rubbed me the wrong way. He came across as such a smooth operator that I suspected he had a hidden agenda. For example, he always drove a new car and seemed to take a lot of pricey vacations. Whenever I expressed any curiosity as to where he got the money for such things, he'd just give me a smug smile and some story about having made good investments. It made me wonder about him."

"But you overlooked all of that and kept him on board?"

"If I fired everyone I didn't like or whose life style I wondered about, we'd lose some good people."

"In this case, you were right to have some doubts about him," Malone said. He then summarized what we'd learned that morning.

When he was done, there was a moment of shocked silence. Mr. Harris and Clarissa both had horrified expressions. The lawyer remained unmoved.

"No one tells the boss anything," she groaned. "I'd have fired him for that little game he was playing with Mia."

"I'm not sure how tolerant I'd be of having a drug user on the staff," Harrison added. "But I'd certainly fire anyone who gave drugs to someone underage."

Clarissa turned to her boss. "I'm sorry, Simon, I should have known this was going on. I promise to be more proactive in the future at investigating employee rumors."

"Not really your fault," Malone interjected. "Most employees don't like to squeal to management, although I expect you'd have been hearing from Mia in a few days if Travis persisted."

"But Holly should have known better," Harris added. "He could have come to me."

"And if you'd done anything, Kelly would have ended up in juvenile detention," said Chance. "Travis really had him over a barrel."

Harris shook his head. "I just find it hard to believe that Lambert was willing to take those kinds of risks with his job."

"You'd be surprised how many guys I meet who get off on the thrill of taking risks. They jeopardize their livelihoods and reputations because they're excited by the game," Malone said. "They're also arrogant enough to think that they can get away with almost anything. Lambert sounds like he fits right in with that group."

Harris leaned across the desk. "But does this get us any closer to finding out who killed Travis? I hired you because I'm convinced that Stormy isn't a murderer, but that's my gut feeling. We'll need more than that to convince the police."

"All I've come up with is evidence that there were other folks who were in conflict with Travis. Some of them with better motives than Stormy's desire to protect her job, but these people have alibis. Also, we need something pretty strong to outweigh the fact that the body was found on her property."

"That suggests that the killer was someone who knew her," said Harris. He turned to me. "Do you have any enemies who would want to frame you for murder."

"No, of course not." I didn't think I had anyone I'd even call a true enemy. Some people like me better than others, but nothing that extreme.

"Do your on-air people have listed phone

numbers?" Malone asked Clarissa.

She shook her head. "We tell them to get an unlisted number. There are too many sick people out there who fixate on folks they see on television."

"Does that mean you think the killer worked here?" asked Harris.

"I'm not sure yet, but I don't think it was a coincidence that Lambert's body ended up under Stormy's side lawn. However, I wouldn't be surprised to find out that Lambert did some drug dealing on the side to some of his upwardly mobile friends. That opens the door to any number of people who might have killed him."

"But it wouldn't explain how he ended up outside my kitchen," I added.

"That's true," said Malone.

"How are you going to find out if he was a drug dealer?" asked Clarissa.

"The police will have been through his apartment by now. I'll check with a friend of mine on the force and see what they've found. But I think I'll also go over there and have a look for myself. You never know what you'll see when you examine things with an open mind."

Mr. Price cleared his throat loudly and looked at me.

"So you have no idea why Travis Lambert's body was found on your property?" he asked me sternly, as though I might have been lying.

"I have no idea."

"And you and Mr. Lambert were not in the custom of meeting outside work?"

I shook my head. Deciding it was time to be fully

honest, I said, "Travis and I did not get along very well, so we were certainly not going to see each other outside of the office."

"Why didn't you get along?" asked Mr. Harris. He seemed disappointed that his people were not one happy, congenial family.

"Travis was angry because I was getting more fan appreciation that he was."

"Were you aware of this conflict?" Mr. Harris asked Clarissa

She shook her head and shrugged. "But how am I supposed to be unless people come to me with information?" she said, looking accusingly at me.

"How did you know he was angry with you?" asked Mr. Price. "Did he tell you?"

"He threatened me. He said that unless I left the station, he was going to make my life miserable."

"Did he ever act on this?" the lawyer asked.

"One night my entire broadcast was mysteriously erased from the computer. I had to give the entire report with no visuals or cue cards."

"But do you know this was the fault of Mr. Lambert?" Price asked.

"I don't know for certain. But that day Travis stayed around long after his work was over, and he was seen going into the broadcast room."

Price cleared his throat. "So you can't say for sure what happened?"

"No," I admitted, barely keeping my anger under control. "But that was the thing about Travis, he was cunning and sneaky. He warned me he could get me fired, and no one would ever suspect him."

The lawyer gave me a bland stare.

"Should I be looking for a criminal attorney?" I asked.

Price pursed his lips.

"Surely, you can handle this for her, Harvey?" Harris said.

"I don't think that would be wise. I might have a conflict of interest depending on how things turn out. I am the station's counsel first and foremost. If Ms. McCloud's interest should turn out to be opposed to that of the station, I would be in a bind."

"So what should I do?"

"If this goes any further, I would advise you to hire your own attorney."

"What do you mean by *goes any further*?" I asked.

"If they should call you in for more questioning or prefer charges."

"You mean charge me with Travis' murder?"

He nodded.

That sinking feeling in the pit of my stomach returned. I needed to get out of the room and go somewhere alone where I could think.

"Don't worry," Harris said to me with a sympathetic smile. "Things may never get that far."

He glanced over to Price for support, but the man remained impassive.

"Are you feeling well enough to go on the air today?" Harris asked me.

The last thing I felt like doing was standing on the set talking to tens of thousands of people about the weather. What I wanted to do was curl up in a ball and stay there until this all blew over. But this was one of those times when I had to prove I was tough enough to do the job under any conditions.

"Of course I can go on," I said in a defiant tone.

"Good. I knew we could count on you," Harris said.

"But do we even want her on the air?" Clarissa said. "The newspaper and other television stations are going to get ahold of this story by tomorrow. If we keep her on the air, it could be damaging to the station."

I glared at Clarissa. *If you had been more on top of your personnel, none of this would have happened*, I wanted to say but didn't.

Simon shook his head. "If we keep her off the air, it will be like an admission of her guilt. I'm hoping that we'll find out that this murder had nothing to do with the station at all. If the murder gets solved fast and leaves Stormy in the clear—as, of course, it will—this whole episode will be quickly forgotten."

Clarissa clearly wanted to say more, but pursed her lips and remained silent. Price was studying a spot on the floor as if it held some kind of answer. Chance gave me a small smile. Only Harris, Chance, and I held out any hope that this would work out well for me. And I wasn't all that sure of it myself.

Harris got to his feet and reached over to shake Malone's hand. "I can see that some pretty ugly things about this station might come to light as a result of your investigation. I'd rather that this information didn't have to become public, but if it's necessary to clear Stormy, then so be it."

Harris looked at me and nodded. I gave him a genuine smile of appreciation.

"Glad to hear you say that," Malone said. "Because that's the way I work. By the way, do you have any policy prohibiting workers from dating?"

Harris glanced at Clarissa. "We're not that draconian or paternalistic, are we?"

"Of course not."

"Interesting," Malone said.

Chapter Eight

"Can you give me a few more moments of your time?" Malone asked me once we had left Mr. Harris' office. "I'd like to talk to the studio people before I go."

"Sure, they're right across the hall. I'll introduce you." Then I asked the question that was burning a hole in my mind. "So why do you think Travis lied to Debbie about the rules on dating?"

"Oh, the usual reason. He wanted to keep their affair private so he could play around. Our boy had several games going at the same time."

We went into the studio, and I introduced Malone to Maggie and Ray. It was funny, but for a moment I was able to see them through Chance's eyes. Maggie was a maternal looking woman appearing to be near forty but probably, in reality, much younger, wearing big glasses, a T-shirt, and oversized jeans, while Ray with his T-shirt, ripped pants, and overlong hair looked like someone who had just been taken in off the street.

Malone made a point of shaking hands with each of them. Then he explained who he was and why he'd been hired.

"Good!" said Maggie. "I'm glad that Simon is looking after Stormy. I'm sure she had nothing to do with the Travis murder."

"Who do you think might have?" asked Malone.

"We didn't have much to do with him," Maggie

explained. "He worked the morning shift, and we only come on in the afternoon. We knew him a little but not enough to say why anyone would hate him enough to kill him."

"That Lambert dude could be a pain," Ray added. "I worked double shifts for a while when they were looking to hire another cameraman, so I was on mornings, too. Lambert was always wanting me to shoot him from his good side like the guy had a good side."

"But he wasn't as much of a prima donna as his predecessor," Maggie said.

"Yeah, I remember him. I only worked with him for a little while, but he was a real prize." Ray frowned. "Bob Toby, that was his name. He was real handsome in an arrogant, shove-it-in-your-face kind of way. But that dude got his in the end, too."

"Was he murdered?" Malone asked, surprised.

"Nah, something even better," Ray said. "The dude went into a hardware store to buy a snow shovel on a stormy day that he had predicted would be fair and mild. He should have known better. He was recognized by a viewer, and before long an angry mob of guys materialized around the checkout counter demanding to know how he could have been so wrong. Most weathermen would have apologized, but not Bob. He told them all where they could put their snow shovels, then vaulted over the counter and raced across the parking lot toward his car. He would have made it except someone came skidding in at sixty miles an hour and clipped him. The mob was still standing there in the unpredicted gale force winds threatening him as he was lying on the ground moaning in pain when the police arrived. He was lucky he wasn't murdered."

"What happened to him?" I asked. Being confronted by one angry member of the public was every meteorologist's worst nightmare. Poor Bob Toby had experienced that in spades.

"He moved to Ohio," said Maggie.

"The dude was never the same after his leg healed. He was afraid of the camera because he pictured the angry mob on the other side of it," Ray said, his prominent Adam's apple bobbing up and down at the humor of it all. "I think he went into something technical like computers."

"But you don't think Travis was killed by an angry viewer?" asked Malone.

"No, of course not," Maggie replied. "He was pretty popular. Anyway, folks don't actually kill weathermen when they get it wrong. They just complain about it a lot."

"Some folks have suggested that the murder could have something to do with Travis' drug connections?" Malone said.

I liked the way he attributed an unsupported speculation of his own to a vague someone else.

"We don't know anything about that, dude," Ray said a shade too quickly.

"He's right,' Maggie added. "Travis kept pretty quiet about his personal life around here. We suspected he used some stuff himself, but nobody talked about it. As long as it didn't interfere with his work on camera, we weren't going to report him to management."

"Yeah, don't ask, don't tell, that's our motto," said Ray with a grin as if he had invented the phrase.

Malone handed each of them a business card and

urged them to give him a call if they came up with any new ideas, no matter how far out.

As we walked into the hall, Malone turned to me.

"They seem like good people to work with."

"The best. They're the ones who make me look good on camera."

"Oh, I don't think you need much help to look good."

I let the compliment slide. Compliments from handsome men don't impress me much. They just remind me of my mother's boyfriend, another handsome guy who knew how to talk his way around anybody in a dress.

"Any more investigating on tap for today?" I asked.

"I'd like to talk with Mia once more to see if she has a list of employees' addresses."

I accompanied him to the front desk where he gave Mia another winning smile that got an equally delighted smile in return.

"One last question, do you have a list of employees' addresses?"

"Right here," she said, holding up a clipboard. "Addresses and phone numbers."

"Would that be common knowledge?"

"That I have the list? Oh sure, people use it all the time to send cards and stuff. Everyone knows it's here. They can just come and look for themselves."

"Can you remember anyone taking a look at the list over the past few days?"

Mia shook her head. "But the list is always hanging right here. Somebody could come by and take a look even when I'm not at my desk."

Malone nodded, looking solemn.

"Is that like a clue of some kind?" Mia asked.

"It could be," Malone said, giving her another smile.

I grabbed his arm when we reached the front door of the station.

"What were you getting at back there?"

"Just that anyone who works here could have found out where you lived."

"And that includes Travis."

"Right."

"But why would he be lurking around my house?"

"As I said, when we learn that we'll be a long way toward solving this case."

We said goodbye, and I watched him walk across the parking lot. He crossed paths with Lieutenant Green coming in with a couple of officers. I heard Malone say hello. He got a grim nod in return. I didn't stay by the front door to be the first to chat with the police. I turned around and scurried back to my desk.

I had just sat down again when my phone rang.

"Hi," Gloria said when I answered. "I heard about Travis on the news. That's terrible. I know you didn't like him much, but still…"

Gloria is my best friend in town. She works in real estate, and that's how we met. I went to her to find a rental, and she put me in touch with Bud McDonald. Gloria is single, so we sometimes go out to bars and clubs. But most of the time we just get together for lunch.

"What are they saying on the news about where the body was found?" I asked.

"Just that it was in a quiet suburban street here in

town, nothing more specific than that. Why does it matter?"

I explained that he had been discovered in my yard. With Gloria, the words usually came tumbling out in a happy profusion. The silence with which she greeted my information told me a lot.

"How could that happen?" she finally asked.

"I have no idea, and I mean it. I had nothing to do with Travis' murder."

"I never thought you did, not even for a minute."

"Thanks."

"Although lord knows he gave you nothing but trouble."

"That's why it looks so bad for me," I said and explained how I had come to be the number one suspect.

"How can they believe that you would bash someone's head in with a rock? To do that a person would have to be crazy with anger at the guy."

"He made me afraid and angry sometimes, but never enough to be that furious. You're right, it would take a lot of emotion to kill someone that way."

"Have the police charged you with anything yet?"

I explained to Gloria how Malone and I were conducting our own investigation.

"Well, I hope you come up with something. But if the police keep hounding you, maybe you'd better get yourself a good lawyer."

I agreed that I would, and we talked about getting together for lunch in a couple of days. Gloria ended by encouraging me to get out more, and not to sit around at home and brood. I promised her I wouldn't, but anywhere I went I would probably bring my brooding right along with me.

After we hung up, I sat and looked across the bullpen. The police team had divided up, and I could see the two officers who had come with Lieutenant Green were talking to Holland Finch. The best I could hope for was that they would find out that other people were having troubles with Travis besides myself. But I was pretty sure that wouldn't get me off the hook as their main suspect.

Nothing Chance and I had discovered so far was going to do that.

Chapter Nine

I lay alone in my house wide-awake, alert to every sound. The windows and doors were carefully locked and had been double and triple-checked. I had drawn all the shades and even placed my old softball bat within handy reaching distance of the bed. It was only with great effort that I'd managed to put out the lights. But now I lay there, knowing that sleep wouldn't come. All I kept thinking was that someone had been murdered right outside my house.

I strained my ears, wondering if I could tell normal from abnormal sounds. The loud rumble of the furnace fan, which I'd always liked in the past because it provided a kind of white noise that helped me sleep, now seemed dangerous because it would also conceal the sounds of anyone trying to break in. I debated with myself whether to shut off the heat, but my own weather report had forecast below freezing temperatures during the night. Grimly admitting that sleep wasn't going to come, I walked into the kitchen without turning on the lights to get a glass of water.

I was standing by the sink wondering how long I should stay up when a beam of light flashed across the window in front of me. Involuntarily I ducked, even though the window shade was down. I froze for a long moment, squatting down behind the counter, trying to figure out what to do. Finally deciding that it was safe to stand, I reached over and gradually pulled back the edge of the shade to peek out. At first, I saw nothing but darkness. But as I stepped away and angled my view closer to the house, I could make out a beam of light carefully surveying the rock garden along the back wall. Someone was out there. Was it the killer returning to try to find the rock he used to murder Travis? That hardly made sense. Even the stupidest killer would know that the police had already searched the area for that. But whatever his reason for being there, someone should be notified. If they caught the killer, I'd be off the hook.

My first instinct was to call 911, but the prospect of dealing with Lieutenant Green again had no appeal. He'd probably accuse me of inventing a mystery man just to divert suspicion from myself, which now that I came to think about it wasn't a half-bad idea. Instead of calling Green, I returned to my bedroom and, using a flashlight, found Malone's card on my dresser. I punched his number into my cell phone. He answered immediately. Although it was well after midnight, there wasn't any sound of sleepiness in his voice as I explained the situation.

"I'll be right there," Malone said. "I was just finishing up some paperwork at the office, so I'm only ten minutes away. Are you sure all the doors and windows are locked?"

"Definitely. Should I call the police?"

"Call them about ten minutes from now. That way they can arrive as backup. Otherwise, they might show up with sirens blaring and scare the guy away."

I went into my bedroom and got dressed. I chose a black sweater and matching pants, the perfect ensemble for blending with the night. After the right amount of time had gone by I called the police. They promised to send a car over immediately. Then I parked myself by the front window to keep on the lookout for Malone. A few minutes later I saw a car park half a block up the street from the house. I saw a figure get out of the car and work his way down the street, staying close to the fronts of the houses and outside the puddles of light made by the street lamps. When he reached the front of my house, he stood for a moment then slipped around the side where I lost sight of him. That had to be Malone.

Now I had a choice. I could sit here and wait to see what the outcome of this adventure was going to be, or I could go outside and be part of it myself. Just like I hadn't wanted Malone to carry on his interrogations without me, for the same reason I wasn't going to leave him to confront this intruder alone. I slipped out the front door and followed him around the side of the house. He was at the back corner standing very still. As I watched, he went around the corner, moving very slowly. I followed, keeping about ten feet behind. I turned the corner. Another ten feet in front of me I could see a large figure bending over and examining the ground as if he were a nighttime gardener.

Malone edged along, clearly hoping to creep close enough to get the jump on him. But a snapped twig brought the flashlight up and caught Malone in the beam. Malone must have figured he had no options left because he charged forward. A few feet before he reached the man his feet went out from under him on the wet grass. He slid hard into the intruder right at knee level, like a runner sliding into second base to break up a double play. The force of the contact sent the man up in the air over Malone, and he landed with an audible groan about six feet in front of me. Malone picked up the flashlight and directed it at him. I saw the man reach in his pocket and pull out something that he pointed at Malone. It was a gun.

If I had paused to think, I probably never would have done it. But instinctively I rushed forward and ran into the intruder, grabbing his gun arm and shaking it hard. For a moment, we did a sort of feverish tango. Then he threw me off, and I fell to the ground. This was it. Chance and I were both going to end up dead. The intruder must have decided that two was one too many because he immediately turned around and began to run across the lawn and up the street. Malone gave chase but lost his footing once again on the wet lawn. A few seconds later, I heard a car screeching away from the curb.

I got to my feet, and dizziness made me wobble. Malone's arms were around me before I could fall.

"Are you okay?" he asked.

I nodded and waved a hand weakly. "Just a little shaken up. That was like running into a cement truck."

"Yeah, he was big and fast, too. That was a risky thing to do. What were you thinking?"

"Oh, I don't know. Maybe I just didn't want another dead body in my yard quite so soon."

"What are you talking about?"

"He had a gun."

Using the flashlight, Malone began searching the area around us. As he walked along, he kicked something hard on the ground in front of him. The flashlight beam revealed a gun lying at his feet. He carefully picked it up with his handkerchief. I figured he was trying to preserve prints.

"So this is what he pointed at me. I couldn't tell at the time. It looks like you may have saved my life," he said, showing the gun to me. "I guess I'm glad you took that risk."

"A Glock pistol," I said in a voice that sounded odd even to me. Suddenly I felt very exposed standing out here in the dark. The sensation that someone was watching me crept up my spine and made me shiver. "I think I'd like to go in now."

I stumbled slightly as I began to walk. Malone put an arm around me and assisted me into the house. Once inside I sank down on the sofa.

"Would you like a cup of tea?" Malone asked, looking at me with concern. I nodded.

He went into the kitchen, and I could hear him searching for things. I was being a bad hostess. I should go help him, but I couldn't find the strength to climb to my feet. Instead, I closed my eyes and the next thing I knew Malone was standing in front of me with a steaming cup of tea. I took a couple of sips and smiled at Malone who was now sitting on the occasional chair across from the sofa.

"I don't know what's wrong with me."

"You were on an adrenaline high and just came crashing down. It happens to everyone. Plus a lot of people tougher than you would feel the same way after having a brush with death."

Brush with death, somehow that phrase didn't make me feel any better.

"You did a very brave thing out there, charging into that big guy like that, especially when you saw he had a gun. Not many women, or men either for that matter, would have rushed into the fight. Of course, I don't know how I'll ever live it down."

"Live what down?"

"Being saved by a female client. That doesn't help my hard-boiled detective image."

I gave him a long look and decided that he really didn't seem all that embarrassed by what I had done. I figured there were a lot of men who wouldn't be so willing to accept having been saved by a woman with such good grace.

Malone's expression turned grim "We were very lucky this time."

"Not lucky enough. He got away."

"My fault, and I'm not happy about it."

There was a knock on the door and a voice called out, "Police."

"I'm sure they won't be pleased, either," he added.

****

Over an hour later, the police left with a final warning that Lieutenant Green would no doubt want to speak with both of us in the morning. Malone had given them the Glock and a rough physical description of the man, but the only chance of identification would depend on whether there were any fingerprints on the weapon and whether those fingerprints were in the law enforcement system.

Once the police left, Malone sat for a moment with a pensive expression.

"What's wrong?" I finally asked.

"I find it odd that the guy was so professional."

"Why?"

"Well, the murder of Travis seemed to be a kind of

spur of the moment thing. Somebody got in a fight with him and bashed him over the head with a rock. But the guy who was out there tonight was armed. I think if he killed Travis it would have been with a bullet or a knife, not a rock that he happened to find on the ground."

"So are you saying that the person we tangled with tonight isn't the person who killed Travis?"

"That's the way it seems to me."

"Then who was he?"

"Someone else who was involved in Travis' rather messy life, no doubt. We'll find out if we keep digging."

I looked around the room, and suddenly I wanted to be anywhere but here. Maybe tomorrow night I'd feel strong enough to sleep in my bed, but right now I wanted to go someplace else. I told Malone how I felt.

"I could sleep on the couch here in the living room if it would make you feel safer."

I shook my head. "I'd like to be somewhere else. Somewhere that no one expects me to be."

"You could come to my apartment. No funny business," he added quickly. "I have a spare bedroom."

"Thanks. I know it sounds odd, but I think I'd feel safer if I were alone. I could check into a motel, but doing that at this hour of the night feels kind of creepy. Plus if I were recognized, a rumor could get started."

"Well, there is my office."

"Sleeping in your office chair with my feet up on the desk doesn't sound very comfortable."

Malone smiled. "It's worked fine for me lots of times. But actually, I have a roll out bed. It's not very plush, but I can promise clean sheets and even supply a coffee maker."

"And you'd let me stay there by myself?"

"Why not?" He grinned. "All my files are locked."

"Is the neighborhood safe?"

"You're letting your television stereotype of a private eye fool you. My office is over a laundry. It might be a little hot in the summer, but the neighborhood is perfectly respectable."

I gave it some thought.

"So do we have a deal?" Malone asked. "You can follow me over in your car, so you can leave before I arrive in the morning if you like. It even has its own bathroom. Sorry, I can't provide a shower, but it's a lot cheaper than staying in a motel. And hopefully less creepy."

I smiled at his sales job. "Thanks, you've got a deal. Let me just throw a few things together, and I'll be ready to go," I said heading into the bedroom.

When I came into the living room a few minutes later, Malone was sort of wandering around the rooming doing a mental inventory.

"So what do you think of the place?"

"You want the truth?"

"Of course."

"The room lacks a lot of the accessories I associate with a woman's apartment. There are no knickknacks or photos covering the surfaces of the two tables. Even the furniture is minimal, a leather sofa with a matching chair."

"Less is more. It makes the space seem larger."

"I'm just wondering whether the absence of stuff is due to having only lived here a few months or whether it reflects a more general philosophy of life."

"What would I find if I went to your apartment?"

He chuckled. "Something very much like this. Aside from the necessary office equipment and some basic furniture purchased from charity shops, I don't own much that I couldn't fit in my car. I learned to travel light in the army. Plus I have a recurring fantasy where I put all my essential belongings in the car and head west."

"What would you do out west?"

Malone grinned. "Probably the same thing I'm doing here. That's why I haven't bothered to make the trip."

"I guess I like to travel light, too."

He nodded. "I have one thing you don't."

"What's that?"

"Pictures of my family. You don't seem to have any. Didn't you move back into the area to be closer to your family?"

"Sort of."

He looked at me expectantly.

"Maybe this is like you explaining why you became a detective. We'll put it on the back burner until the case is over."

I turned away, grabbed my small overnight bag, and headed for the door.

"Just one more question before we go," Chance said.

"What's that?"

"How did you know that gun was a Glock? I knew, but I'm supposed to know."

"My father insisted that I learn to shoot for self-protection. At least that's what he claimed. I think it was because he'd really wanted a son. I always used a Glock, so I recognized it right away."

"Do you own a gun?"

"I shook my head. My father wanted me to have one, but I don't always do what he wants."

Malone seemed to know by the tone of my voice that the conversation was getting into dangerous territory because he silently escorted me out the door.

Chapter Ten

I followed Chance for the couple of miles it took to get to his office. We parked in a lot behind a small row of businesses, where he unlocked the door to a back stairway that led to his office. The only indication that a private investigator was upstairs came from a small sign by the door reading *Acme Investigations.*

"You're not easy to find," I said as we hoofed up the narrow stairs.

"Most people don't window shop for a private investigator. They call first, and I tell them how to get here. Another reason for being discreet is that folks don't really want to be seen coming out of an investigator's office."

"I suppose a wife who suspected her husband of cheating wouldn't want to advertise her suspicions," I said in a kind of jokey voice.

"No, she wouldn't," he replied in a solemn tone. When we reached the landing, he turned to face me. "Is this going to develop into one of your diatribes about how sleazy my profession is, and how I spend my time peering into bedrooms? Because I want you to consider whether a woman with three kids, whose husband is having an affair with his secretary, should know the truth? I happen to think that she should. Whether she tries to save the marriage or gets a divorce is her choice. But I don't think she should be going along, working hard at the marriage, while her husband is cheating on her. My job is to give her the truth. After that, it's between her, God, and her lawyer what she decides to do with it. So I'm not going to make any apologies for my profession."

"Wow!" I said. "Like you asked me yesterday, where is all that coming from?"

Chance ran a hand over his forehead. "Sorry, it's late, I'm tired, and I don't like having a gun pointed at me."

There was more to it than that. No guy liked to have his job ridiculed.

He walked down the hall, stopped in front of a door on the right, and inserted a key in a deadbolt lock. We went inside. The first office was a reception area. There was no desk. A half-dozen straight back chairs and a couple of stock paintings created a simple waiting room.

"I don't have enough business to need a receptionist. Don't really need a waiting room for that matter, but I had to do something with the space."

His voice was calm and pleasant again. To my relief, his burst of anger seemed to have disappeared as quickly as it had begun. He opened the door to a large back room that had a desk in the center. Across from the desk were a couple of comfortable looking upholstered chairs; I also spotted a computer, a fax machine, and a copier.

"This is where all the magic happens," he said with a grin.

"Do you get a lot of information by doing computer searches?"

"For some cases, that's about all you do. Others

you have to rely on old-fashioned legwork."

Chance opened a closet door and pulled out the trundle bed.

"It's a lot more comfortable than it looks," he assured me, unfolding it. He pulled a pile of folded bedding down from the closet shelf.

"I'll make the bed up later," I said.

"The coffee machine is here." Chance pointed to a shelf behind the desk. He pulled open another door next to the closet. "Here's the sink and toilet."

"Looks like everything I need."

"If you should need some spiritual comfort, it's in the top drawer on the right."

"What's that? A bottle of scotch?"

Chance smiled. "You're still working with the old stereotype of the hard boiled P.I."

"You mean every private detective doesn't keep a bottle of liquor in his desk to unwind with after a tough day on the trail of the bad guys?"

"I keep a Bible."

"Oh." I stared at him for a moment, waiting for him to wink and say gotcha. When that didn't happen, I felt embarrassed as I always did when people talked about religion. Like politics and one's sex life, in my opinion, it wasn't a proper subject to discuss in public.

"I see," I went on lamely.

"Most of the time I read it for peace and comfort. But to be honest, sometimes when a case has me stumped, I just open the Bible and point to a passage at random. You'd be surprised how often I get an inspiration that helps me solve the case."

"You might want to keep that method to yourself," I suggested. "It sounds a lot like sheer guesswork."

"There is a lot of guesswork in this business. Anyway, I like to think it's my mind interpreting the passage that really solves the case. The Bible just gives me that little spark of inspiration."

I paused. "So do you, like, go to church?"

He nodded. "Do you?"

I shrugged. "I used to go to Sunday school as a little girl."

"When's the last time you went to church?"

"About a year ago. I was a bridesmaid for a friend from college."

"I'm not sure that counts."

"I guess I believe in the things I know to be true, not the things I would like to be true."

"With an open heart and an open mind, you can learn all sorts of new things."

I glanced at the sign on the desk with his name on it and decided to change the subject.

"Can I ask where you got the name *Chance*? Is it a nickname?"

"It's based on my given name. My mother named me Chancellor. I guess she thought I was going to be a politician or an adviser to people in power. As you can imagine, in school it quickly got shortened to Chance. It made a lot more sense back when I was in the army. It kind of fit the lifestyle."

"What did you do in the army?"

His expression closed up as if he didn't want to talk about it.

"Well, I guess I'll leave you now," he said. "Just twist the knob on the deadlock after I leave, and you'll be real secure."

He opened the door then turned back.

"Good night, Stormy."

I smiled at the intimacy. "Good night, Chance."

After he left, I made up the bed. As soon as I turned out the lights, I lay there feeling peaceful and secure. There was something about Chance that made me feel that way. What I appreciated was his easygoing approach to things, so different from my more intense attitude. He was easygoing, but not the irresponsible, frivolous man I had initially thought him to be. I sensed an underlying core of strength in him that a lot of men didn't have.

But then there was this religious side that I had just discovered. Maybe that was the cause of his strength, but religion always made me wary. Never get involved with Bible-thumpers, my father had taught me. They're an irrational, hypocritical lot who think they have all the answers. I was wondering whether Chance in any way fit that description when I drifted off to sleep.

****

The next morning I had finished getting dressed and was wondering whether to go home for breakfast or eat out when there was a knock at the door.

"It's Chance."

I quickly unlocked and opened the door. He stood there with a paper bag in his hand.

"How did you sleep?" he asked, stepping into the office.

"Like a charm. Your office is very restful."

"Especially on warm afternoons. Were you on your way back home?"

"Actually, I was trying to come up with a way to avoid returning there this morning. I guess I'm still a little spooked that I'll find that big man waiting for me.

I was going to go out to breakfast, but couldn't figure out how to manage a change of clothes. I should have put more than a robe, pajamas, and toiletries in my overnight bag."

"How about I take you out to breakfast, then we both go back to your house so you can change?"

"Sounds fine. Thanks."

Chance waved the bag in his hand. "I got up shortly before dawn this morning to take a look at the ground in back of your house. The idea of someone searching there last night got me wondering what he was looking for, so I checked it out in daylight. This is what I found. It was in the middle of a shrub like maybe it had fallen or been thrown there. I only spotted it by accident."

He removed from the bag a statue about five inches tall. It was tan in color and appeared to be carved out of stone. Although the figure had a serene smile on its face, it carried a bow in one hand and a short spear in the other.

"Ever seen it before?" Chance asked.

I took it from him and examined it. "Never. It's very unique, isn't it? It looks old, like the statue of an ancient warrior. I wonder how the police missed finding it?"

"You see what you're looking for. They were looking for a murder weapon, probably a rock, but at any rate, something considerably larger than this. And, like I said, it was down in the middle of a bush. I wonder how it got there. It isn't your usual garden decoration."

"This looks more like a work of art," I said. "You know, I think I might know somebody who could help us identify it. David Palmer teaches art up at the college, and he's director of their art gallery. I met him when he was on the show talking about an art heist in Boston. He even called me yesterday to see how I was holding up and asked if he could be of any help."

"Sounds like our man."

The phone on the desk rang, and Chance answered it. He listened for a long moment without speaking, then rolled his eyes.

"Can we at least have breakfast first?" he asked.

Whatever the response, it must have been brief.

"I see. Well, thank you for your kind offer, Lieutenant."

After hanging up, he turned to me with a frown.

"Sorry, but our breakfast is going to have to wait. As you may have guessed, that was Lieutenant Green, and he'd like to see us, as in now, ASAP, and a number of other expressions that shouldn't be used in polite company. On the positive side, he did offer to give us coffee, although I'm not sure police coffee is any kind of treat."

"Do we have a choice?"

Chance shook his head. "My impression is that we either show up willingly, or we get escorted over there by a couple of officers."

Fifteen minutes later, Chance and I entered the police station and asked for Lieutenant Green. The sergeant at the desk told us to take a seat on the bench in the waiting room. Twenty minutes passed. The sergeant went about his business as if no one was waiting. I became increasingly angry. Police stations didn't provide much reading material, and the wooden bench was hard under my butt.

"Why did Green ask us to hurry if he's too busy to see us?" I complained.

"He's not busy. He's probably in his office reading the sports section," Chance replied. "This is his way of punishing us for not doing things by the book last night."

"What didn't we do by the book?"

"Call the police first and let them try to apprehend the big guy."

"It's petty to get all excited about that," I said angrily.

Chance gave me a warning look. "Better to accept it as part of the game and let it go. Getting all riled up will just put us in more hot water. If Green sees we aren't bothered by all this foolishness, he'll get down to business."

"But I am bothered."

"Of course you are, but don't let it show."

I pursed my lips. "I'll try not to. Don't you have some Bible quotation to cover this sort of thing?"

"Saint Paul says somewhere that patience and the scriptures should give us hope. Is that enough for you?"

"I guess it will have to be. But I can tell you one thing, I'm not telling Green about that statue you found."

"That could be interpreted as concealing evidence."

"Evidence of what? There's no reason to believe that the statue has anything to do with Travis' death. If we tell Green about it, he'll pop it in an evidence bag, and we'll never be able to show it to David. I've got a bad feeling that Green just wants to find me guilty of this whole thing, and that he won't investigate any leads that head in a different direction."

Chance stared at a poster on the other side of the room that warned against phone scams.

"Okay, we'll keep quiet about it at least until your friend gets to take a look at it."

"Thank you," I said, relieved.

"Don't mention it." He gave me one of his dazzling smiles.

My breath caught, and I was sure I blushed down to the roots of my hair. Fortunately, a police officer came along at that moment and took us down the hall. I thought they would put us in separate rooms, but they didn't.

"So, Malone, you had a little tussle with a real criminal last night and came out second best," Green said fifteen minutes later when he finally settled down across the table from us.

While waiting, we'd had ample opportunity to study the walls covered with a textured paint that didn't easily show marks. The room was filled with a table and chairs made of a laminate harder than wood.

"You promised us coffee," Chance said with a thin smile.

"After you tell me everything that happened."

Chance sighed and repeated the events of last evening.

"So, you disarmed this guy. Oh, wait a minute, I meant to say that Ms. McCloud disarmed this guy, and in so doing probably saved your life."

"That's true. By all rights, I should probably be dead."

"Then I'd have another murder to solve, which is one reason we don't like civilians meddling in police business."

"Point taken."

"And then you let him escape. Another reason why Ms. McCloud should have called the police."

I sat there fuming, wanting to say something, but I could tell from the glance Chance gave me that he had this under control.

"She did call the police."

"But not until she phoned her personal knight in shining armor."

"Maybe that's because she feels the police are more interested in arresting her than in protecting her."

"And maybe she and Travis really were having a relationship, and when he wanted to break it off, she killed him. Did you ever consider that?" Green asked, leaning forward until his face was only inches from Chance's.

I took a deep breath, ready to protest my innocence when Chance put a calming hand on my arm.

"There's no evidence that she was involved with Lambert. And you can't have her killing him one day because they were competitors and the next day because they were lovers. You're just guessing."

Green scowled. "So what was the guy with the gun looking for?"

"I have no idea. He obviously thought there was something important back there. What have your people turned up so far?"

Green licked his lips as if uncertain whether to speak. "The murder weapon," he finally announced with a note of triumph.

"Ah. And that would be what—a rock?"

Green appeared to deflate. "A rock from McCloud's garden with Lambert's blood on it."

"A rock which anyone could have used on Lambert," Chance said.

"They didn't get along. The rock was found on her property, and she was home that night. Sounds like motive, means and opportunity to me."

I started to speak, but Chance's hand tightened on my arm.

"Lambert was not a popular guy. As I'm sure you know from your interviews at the station, several people there had as much reason as Stormy to want him dead. And that's leaving aside the folks he knew in the drug trade. That rock was there for anybody to pick up, and you have no proof that Stormy knew Lambert was on her property that night. Go ahead and arrest her. Let Stormy's attorney make a fool of you."

Green paused. "I'm not going to arrest her, not yet. First, I want to find out why Lambert went to her house that night. I've subpoenaed her phone records to see if she had any contact with Lambert earlier that evening to set up a meeting."

"If she planned to kill him, she wouldn't have arranged a meeting at her own house."

I nodded my head vigorously.

"Maybe she expected things to go more smoothly. When they didn't, she suddenly ends up with him dead. Thinking fast she decides to bury him temporarily on the property until she can move the body somewhere for permanent disposal. Unfortunately for her, the work crew showed up the next morning."

"A pretty far-fetched theory, and I still don't think you have enough evidence of motive. Holland and Mia arguably had as much or more reason for wanting to see him dead."

"We're looking into everyone's alibi, don't worry about that. The important thing for you to remember is that you're not a cop. The next time Ms. McCloud calls about a peeping tom, you act like a good citizen instead of a hero wannabe and tell her to call us."

"Will do, Lieutenant," Chance said with a smile.

Green glared at us both for a long moment then left the room. A few minutes later he returned with two paper cups of coffee.

"I keep my promises," he said. "See that you do."

After Green left the room, telling us to wait to be led out, we relaxed and sipped the lukewarm coffee.

"Why did you keep shushing me?" I asked Chance.

"If you said anything, I'm afraid that Green would eventually twist it to use against you. Right now, I'm reasonably confident that Lieutenant Green is too prudent to arrest you without more evidence. Lambert is turning out to be the kind of murder victim who leaves behind a long list of suspects. Something will turn up to show that you don't belong at the head of the line."

"I hope so," I said, still feeling a bit shaken.

Ten minutes later a uniformed officer escorted us out of the interview room.

"Let's get some breakfast," I said as we walked down the front steps of the police station.

The haze of early morning had burned off, and the warm April sun promised a beautiful day. I tried to focus on the positive.

Chance suggested a local coffee shop a few blocks away where he sometimes went for lunch. Since we each had our own car, I followed him. Chance ordered a couple of eggs over easy with bacon, while I, ever aware of my television appearance, went with a single poached egg on toast. I was silent while waiting for breakfast. That must have worried Chance because once the food arrived, he asked, "Did our conversation with Green bother you?"

"Some, but I was a little surprised he didn't say something about our being together so early this morning."

"He was probably thinking about it, but decided to save it for a later time."

"I'm glad you didn't tell him about finding the statue."

"I wouldn't have lied if he'd asked me directly whether I'd found something, but since he didn't ask, I felt no need to volunteer."

"Why wouldn't you lie?"

"It would be stupid to lie to the police. Plus, I just don't lie or at least I try very hard not to. Remember, my job is finding out the truth, and once you start lying, the truth is the first casualty."

"Is this part of that whole religious thing?"

Chance smiled. "I guess, in a way."

"Well, then, I can rely on you to tell me the truth if I ask you something?"

"Fire away."

"Are you sure Lieutenant Green isn't about to arrest me. He gives me the eye like I'm the bird and he's the cat. I keep waiting for him to pounce."

Chance reached across the table and took my hand. "I think you're just one bird in a whole flock right now. Green isn't ready to pounce."

"Good. If I thought he was, I'd follow Mr. Price's advice and hire a good criminal lawyer right away."

"I can give you the names of a couple of the best defense attorneys around, but I don't think you have to contact them quite yet."

I nodded. "So it's not time to panic?"

"Don't worry. I'll let you know if and when that time comes."

I pulled out my cell phone. "Speaking of contacting people, let me see if I can reach David Palmer at the college. Maybe we can go see him right now about the statue if he's free and you have the time."

Chance nodded.

When Palmer answered, he said he'd be happy to see me. As our conversation grew more animated, Chance began to look more and more unhappy.

"He can see us in half an hour at his office. That will just give me time to go home and change."

"Okay," Chance said, handing the waitress some money.

"I'll pay my share."

"My treat," he replied. "Think of it as a form of post interrogation therapy."

"Well, Doc, that was a fine job. A little food and friendly conversation will do it every time."

"Glad to hear it," he said.

Chapter Eleven

After stopping by my house—which turned out not to look all that scary in the light of day—for a change of clothes, we made our way up to Ridley College. Since I'd been there a number of times in the past, I told Chance that I'd lead the way. I pulled in a back entrance and parked behind an old stone building that looked like it must have been one of the first on campus when it was founded in the mid-nineteenth century. Stately trees lined the walk, their leafless branches showing where they had been carefully pruned back so they didn't brush the buildings.

"How come you've been to the college so many times before?" Malone asked. "Did you take classes here?"

"No. I've been here a few times to give presentations in communication courses on meteorology and broadcasting. Plus, I come for the occasional cultural event. I even ran into Travis here a few times at art shows. Do you like concerts and going to museums?"

"Depends on the concert. I don't know much about classical stuff, and I'm pretty ignorant about art."

"You could always learn," I said in an offhand way.

"A tiger doesn't so easily change its stripes," Chance said gruffly like maybe I had offended him.

We went in the side door and up a flight of stairs. The building smelled of age, a damp faintly mildewed aroma that reminded me of old books. At the end of the hall, I stopped in front of a mahogany door and knocked.

"How did you know exactly where his office is?" asked Malone.

"He invited me over from one of the art exhibits to show me a set of prints he had."

Malone gave me a look that I couldn't quite interpret.

David Palmer opened the door and pulled me into a giant hug. To be honest, it was a little more enthusiastic than our past relationship warranted, but it wasn't unpleasant. I'd always found David to be reasonably attractive. In his mid-thirties, he was of average height, slender, and moved with a casual grace. After the introductions, he settled into a chair behind his desk.

"A terrible thing about poor Travis. I hope they catch who did it."

"Did you know Travis?" Malone asked.

"He came to a few exhibits at the art gallery, and, of course, I recognized him from television. Do the police have any idea who did it?"

"Right now I'm the prime suspect because his body was found by my house," I said.

"How did that happen?"

I shrugged. "No one knows. I imagine that once we figure that out, the rest of the story will fall into place."

"Well, whatever the reason for the body being found on your property, I'm sure it will be revealed that the murder had nothing to do with you."

I nodded my thanks and sat back. I felt comfortable

in the office with its two walls covered with books, while a computer monitor stared at us blankly from the top of the desk. It reminded me a bit of my father's study at home.

"Have you read all those?" Malone asked, nodding at the walls.

Palmer smiled. "Most of them."

"That's pretty impressive."

"It's what I do. So I gather you've brought something to show me."

Malone took the statue out of the paper bag and handed it to him. David held it in his palm and began examining it from every angle.

After a few moments, he said, "An interesting piece. I can tell you what it isn't."

"What isn't it?" Malone asked with obvious impatience.

"I don't think it's a work of western art. My guess would be that it comes from India. I'm not familiar with the character being represented, but since most Indian statuary is of gods and goddesses, I would say he represents some divine figure. I might be able to find out if you have a few minutes."

We both nodded, and David pushed a key that brought the computer to life.

From where I was sitting, I could see that he went to an art website and began running a search for Indian religious statuary. The screen filled with pictures of humanlike figures, although as I slid forward more closely to get a better view, I could see that many of them had multiple sets of arms.

"Why the extra arms?" I asked.

"They're considered a sign of power. Some Indian

gods are pictured with several sets."

David leaned forward and began closely studying the images.

"You can often identify the figure by the animal they're with or by the weapons they're holding. Our boy appears to have a bow in one hand and a spear or elephant goad in the other." He paused for a moment then said, "This one is the closest to your statue."

Chance and I hunched over David and stared at the screen.

"Indra, the God of War and the God of Storms," I read. "He sure looks like the statue we've got."

"Indian art isn't my field, but I think Indra is one of the very ancient Hindu gods, going back to the time of the Vedas. He's not a god who is worshipped much today. I could do some further research and let you know more exactly."

"Would this statue be worth much?" Malone asked.

David smiled. "I see you're a man who likes to get right to the bottom line. Again, this isn't my field, but there are lots of statues of Indian gods around. Some are quite ancient, and some are contemporary knockoffs. If authentic, your friend here might sell for a couple of thousand. I doubt he'd be worth much more. Do you mind my asking where you got it?"

I opened my mouth to answer, but Malone interrupted me.

"Sorry, we can't tell you that right now," he said firmly. He reached over and snatched the statue off the desk.

David shrugged. "That's quite all right. We curators are just curious creatures by nature, and we like to stay abreast of what things are available on the market. You never know when someone's private collection is coming up for sale."

"We'll tell you more when we can," I said, trying to smooth over Malone's abruptness.

David turned to me and said, "There's a reception this Sunday afternoon at the gallery for the opening of a local artist's work. If you are free, perhaps we could have brunch together and then go to the reception. The artist's name is Doug Fowler, and he does a lot of interesting things with geometric forms."

I quickly flipped through my mental calendar.

"I'd be delighted," I said.

"Great, I'll give you a call tomorrow and work out the details."

Malone got to his feet. "Thanks for your time, Dr. Palmer."

"Please, call me David."

Malone nodded and shook hands with him. "Thanks again, David, and if you find out anything else about our little friend, let us know.

"Will do." David gave me a parting hug and repeated his intention to give me a call.

"I didn't realize you knew him quite that well," Malone said as we walked across the parking lot to our cars.

"Neither did I, but I guess David is just a very demonstrative kind of guy. He's quite intelligent, too."

"With all those books he's read, he'd have to be."

I gave him a sidelong glance. "You didn't like him."

Malone rattled the car keys in his hand. "I don't know him well enough to say that."

"But you didn't want me to tell him where the

statue came from."

"That was nothing personal against him. The fewer people who know the facts in a criminal investigation, the better off things are. People talk, even when they swear to your face that they won't. Then before long you have the police at your door wanting to know why you're withholding evidence."

"Fair enough," I said. Then another thought occurred to me. "So what do you think, if anything, the god Indra has to do with Travis' death?"

"I'm sure it has something to do with it. To have a dead man and a statue of an ancient god show up in your yard at the same time is too much of a coincidence."

"Travis wasn't a collector as far as I know."

"One statue doesn't make a collection. But I think I'd like to know more about him."

"He's dead. You've already talked to the people he worked with. How are you going to find out any more?"

"I haven't talked to the morning crew who actually worked with him. I think I should do that. But first I'm going to take a look around his apartment."

"Will the police let you in?"

"I have a feeling that I might be able to find a way in without asking their permission. Are you free tomorrow morning to come with me?"

"Around nine?"

Malone nodded and took a couple of steps toward his car before he turned back.

"Would you like me to follow you home from the station tonight? I can check out your house."

That was tempting, very tempting. But I already

felt silly about being afraid to return alone this morning.

"No thanks. I'll be fine. And thanks for coming over last night and for letting me stay at your office."

He gave me a salute. "All part of the service, ma'am."

As I got behind the wheel of my car, I wondered why Malone had seemed kind of distant after our meeting with David. And why had he taken such a dislike toward the man? Could it have been because David asked me out and I accepted? Was Malone jealous? I pushed the idea out of my mind. Guys like Malone who led exciting, active lives, weren't interested in girls like me. They wanted women who were more flamboyant and showy—girls who wanted to party, not sit around and read books. Or if his religious side didn't allow that much frivolity, he'd want a woman who was traditionally docile. I may look like the girl next store, but that's not the way I think. At least with David, you knew exactly what you were getting—a smart, nice man with a secure career in front of him. With that thought in mind, I drove out of the parking lot, keeping a healthy distance between my car and Malone's.

Chapter Twelve

After getting back to the office, I sat at my desk and stared at the computer screen. Weather fronts moved with slow deliberativeness across the country from west to east. I should have been projecting what was going to reach the viewing area over the next few days, but I was finding it hard to concentrate. It was as though all the disturbing events of the last few days had finally begun to hit home. My mind kept spinning, and all I could see was the dead face of Travis Lambert staring up at me from a shallow grave. Whatever Travis had done, whatever Travis had been, he didn't deserve to end up like that. Then there was the added anxiety of knowing that the police still had me at the top of their list for his murder. Unless a more likely suspect turned up soon, I was worried that the pressure on the police to solve a high profile case might lead to my being charged. Even if I were eventually found innocent, the headline Weather Girl Murderer would haunt me for the rest of my life. And no doubt destroy my career.

My phone rang. I picked up, anxious to be distracted from my thoughts.

"Hello, Stormy," my father said. "How are you?"

"Fine," I replied automatically.

My father paused and gave a dry cough, waiting for me to say more.

"How is the police investigation progressing?" he

finally asked.

"They've found several other people who had reason to dislike Travis, but I'm not off the hook."

"Have you gotten a lawyer yet?"

"No, but I will if the police get serious about charging me."

"Tell them nothing without your attorney present. Anything you say can be distorted and used against you in court."

"Hopefully it won't come to that."

"Has that private detective been of any help?"

"Yes." I described his discovery of the statue.

"Do you have any idea as to how this fits in with the murder?"

"Not yet."

"Are you sure you don't want me to come out there? I feel rather helpless being so far away."

"I don't think there's any advantage to your being here right now. But there was one thing I've been wondering about."

"What's that?"

"For some reason, I've been thinking a lot about my past lately. Probably it has to do with being under a lot of stress. I seem to remember going to Sunday School when I was a little girl, but I stopped around the time Mom left us. Am I right?"

"Odd you should be thinking about that. But you remember correctly. Your mother was always the churchgoer in the family, strange for someone who was in many ways such a free spirit. But she was the emotional one. I've always thought religious belief is not adequately supported by evidence. But we agreed that you would be exposed both to religion and to a more scientific approach to life. Then it would be up to you to decide."

"What happened to that plan?"

"When your mother left us, I guess I tried to forget about all the things having to do with her, and going to church was one of them. So I'm afraid I never gave you the opportunity to see both sides. Do you think that's done you any harm?"

"I don't know."

"Yes, of course, how could you?"

"Well, maybe once my immediate problems are settled, I'll try experimenting with religion."

My father laughed. "It might be too late. All the years of living with me has probably inoculated you against the disease of religion."

"I guess we won't know until I've actually been exposed. You're not opposed to my finding out?"

"Not at all. As I get older, I sometimes think that I've been too stubborn."

"You're not stubborn, you just believe what you believe."

"Yes, but one shouldn't be inflexible. You have to stay open to opposing points of view." He paused, but I remained silent. It was rare to hear my father express self-doubts. "I sometimes think that I was too stubborn in not forgiving your mother and taking her back."

"But she ran off with another man."

"Yes, well maybe we were both a bit to blame for that. I was so caught up in my career I neglected her, and that other man could be very persuasive. Even I liked him when we first met before everything else happened."

"I don't think you were wrong to make a complete

break with Mom."

"Maybe not wrong, but not completely right. All those years lost when she was the only one for me. It seems a shame. All I've managed to do is ruin two lives—maybe three."

"You didn't ruin mine. You brought me up just fine."

"It would have been better if you'd had a mother. I've always been aware of what I couldn't give you. How would you feel about having a mother now?"

"What?" Now I was truly confused. "What are you talking about?"

"My getting in touch with your mother again. It's never too late. How would you feel about that?"

"I don't know." I paused and took a deep breath. "I really don't know. I guess that's up to you."

"I wouldn't do it without your permission."

"Do it then, if you think it's right for you."

He didn't say anything for a long moment. "Well, back to this other thing, if you need my help don't hesitate to ask for it. I'll be there in a flash. I know you are a smart, capable woman, but this is a lot for any one person to handle alone."

After thanking my father and hanging up, my mind wandered. Why I had moved back to this area? If it was to reconnect with my father, I was certainly doing a poor job of it, since I had only seen him twice in the last five months. I had no old friends from high school whom I longed to see, and although this was a marginally bigger television market than the one in Pennsylvania, it wasn't a dramatic improvement career-wise. So why was I here?

Maybe it did have something to do with hoping to

be part of a family again. I had returned to the area where I had at least been part of a truncated family composed of my father and myself, but I had remained reluctant to reach out to him. Now it seemed like my family might be complete again, and I didn't know how I felt about that.

Deciding I wasn't going to come up with an answer to the question right now, I went down the hall to the break room. I found some orange juice that wasn't past its sell-by date and poured myself a glass, hoping the sugar would get my brain back on track. I was sitting at one of the small round tables when Debbie came in and poured a cup of the inky black coffee that had probably been on the burner since this morning.

"Mind if I join you?" Debbie asked.

"Sure," I replied, not really wanting to talk to her but unable to avoid it without being insulting.

Debbie settled into the plastic chair across from me. "I just wanted to ask how things are going with the investigation."

"I don't know what Malone would say, but right now I don't think we've got any idea who killed Travis, and I don't think the police are doing any better."

"That's a shame. Are you still a suspect?"

My high-pitched laugh sounded close to the edge even to my own ears.

"Since the body showed up in my yard, I guess I am. But aside from the fact that Travis occasionally threatened to get me fired if I showed him up, I don't think I had much of a motive."

"Travis' bark was always worse than his bite. I don't think he would actually have attempted to get you fired."

I wasn't about to accept this naughty-puppy-dog view of Travis. To me, he was a pit bull.

"Since you and Travis were going out together, I guess you have feelings for him. But, if you'll forgive me for saying so, I think that maybe you had a more positive view of him than he deserved."

I'd half-expected Debbie to get angry at the suggestion that she had overestimated Travis, but instead, she looked thoughtful.

"You may be right," she finally said, sipping her coffee. "But you have to understand that I knew him better than anyone else. He had a horrible home life and was basically an insecure guy who needed constant support and encouragement. He got all of that from the public before you came along. As you became more popular, his confidence was undermined. That's why he came on so tough with you. He was frightened."

Bad home life sounded like the justification for every serial killer who'd ever lived.

"I may understand why he did it, but that still doesn't make it right."

"I don't think he could help himself."

I had reservations about giving him quite so much benefit of the doubt, but instead of saying anything, I took another sip of my orange juice. I glanced around the room at the hard plastic surfaces bathed in the harsh fluorescent light and thought how similar our break room was to a police interrogation room. I decided that maybe I should take advantage of that similarity of ambience to question Debbie some more.

"You told us before that you'd been going out with Travis for about six weeks?"

"That's right."

"But you kept it secret."

"Until Hildie saw us last weekend and told everyone."

"And you kept it secret because Travis told you Mr. Harris had a rule against co-workers dating?"

"That's right."

"But when Malone and I asked Mr. Harris whether there was such a rule, he denied it."

Debbie frowned. "Well, I guess Travis had his own reasons," she replied easily.

Sure, I thought, like he wanted to stay free to play the field. To go on intimidating Mia and any other vulnerable female who came along.

"Actually, there was another reason," Debbie went on. "Travis had been going out with someone before me who he said was the jealous, emotional type. So he wanted to keep things quiet until he'd had a chance to gently break it off with her."

"Did he ever tell you who this other woman was?"

Debbie shook her head. "He told me that he wasn't the kind of guy to kiss and tell. He believed that past relationships should remain private. Caring about other people's feelings was one of the things I loved about him. I really thought we could make it work for the long run."

I nodded, Travis was probably most concerned with protecting himself. In fact, I doubted whether there was another woman at all. Travis probably just wanted to keep his affair with Debbie a secret for his own purposes. As for Debbie's long run prospects, I was pretty sure that Travis didn't want to be tied down in Ridley. He was always sending out his demo tape. If an opportunity presented itself in Boston or Chicago, he'd make tracks and be travelling solo.

"Did Travis collect things?"

"What kind of things?" Debbie asked, puzzled.

"Little statues or figurines."

"I've only been to his apartment two or three times because we usually went to my place, but I don't remember anything like that. Why do you ask?"

"Just something the police questioned me about," I said, mentally crossing my fingers at the lie and figuring they certainly would have asked me about it if I had mentioned it to them.

"I don't think he was interested in interior decorating. His place was pretty simple. Just like you'd expect a bachelor's apartment to be. I would have offered to help him decorate, but we hadn't reached that stage yet." Tears welled up in her eyes at the thought of what might have been.

I took a swallow of my orange juice and decided our conversation needed a bracing burst of honesty.

"What about his drug dealing? Did he ever discuss that with you?"

Debbie smiled, unfazed. "Travis didn't deal drugs. Oh, he used the stuff once in a while and might have sold some to a friend now and then, but he was no dealer. I certainly didn't approve of even his limited involvement. I wouldn't put any of that poison in my body. I tried to talk him out of using it, and given more time, I'm certain that I would have been successful."

"So you don't think he was dealing on the side?"

She shook her head vehemently.

"It's just that none of us gets paid all that well, so I was wondering if he had any other work."

"He told me that he worked in construction for a

while when he first came to the station. He worked on rehab projects. He had a lot of school debts he was trying to pay off."

"How did he afford the fancy car and the nice vacations?"

"He told me that he made smart investments and saved a lot. We were planning to go on a cruise in the summer. I offered to pay my own way, but Travis insisted that he could easily afford to pay for both of us. He was always generous."

I nodded, deciding that there wasn't much more to learn from Debbie. She clearly had her own idealized picture of Travis, and I was finding it painful listening to her relive her dreams.

"Well, I guess I'd better get back to work. I'm on air in fifteen."

I got to my feet and headed for the door.

"I hope either that detective of yours or the police find out what happened to Travis. He was too nice a guy to die like that."

I didn't trust myself to speak. *Nice guy* were certainly not the words I would have used to describe Travis. I considered how similar Travis must have been to the guy who seduced my mother. Both charming when they wanted to be, both attractive to women, and both able to sell dreams based on promises they wouldn't fulfill. My heart went out to Debbie. Only Travis' untimely death had prevented her from being hurt, just as my mother had been. I hoped the solution to the case wouldn't leave Debbie more upset than she already was.

No sooner had I gotten back to my desk than my cell phone rang. It was Gloria.

"How about we firm up that luncheon date," she said. "I've been out of town for the last couple of days, and today I'm trying to catch up. Why don't we get together for lunch tomorrow."

"As long as I'm back at work by two."

"Let's meet at The Lunch Wagon at high noon?"

"I look forward to it."

Several minutes later I went across the hall to the studio and did my mid-afternoon weather highlight. When I finished, and Ray had drifted down the hall for another cup of coffee, Maggie drew me to one side.

"Any results in finding out what happened to Travis?" she asked, her eyes large behind her glasses.

I shook my head. I was getting tired of responding to the questions when there was nothing positive to be said. When Maggie kept staring at me, I could tell she expected more.

"Malone and the police are doing all they can. I think the most plausible theory is that drugs were involved. If that's true, we may never know who killed him. Of course, that doesn't explain why he was at my house when he died. Until we have an answer to that, I'm afraid the police are going to be focusing on me."

Maggie nodded and rolled up the sleeves on her faded denim shirt. As usual, she was aggressively dressed down—baggy jeans, an oversized shirt, and glasses harking back to the seventies.

Did Maggie have any kind of social life? Of course, working from two in the afternoon until eleven at night didn't help me or anyone else get dates. When most people were off, we were working. We did get most Saturdays and Sundays, although even there we had to work one weekend a month. But I had a feeling that in Maggie's case, even if she had more free time, devotion to her job would keep her from having many friends outside work.

"Well, I have no idea why Travis was out at your place that night," Maggie said. "But I've been thinking that there might have been someone else who had it in for Travis around here."

"Who's that?"

"Clarissa's husband, Slobo."

Slobodan Krankovich, Clarissa Hayes' husband, was known to be a minority owner of the station, so, of course, the word was that he had been influential in getting her the job as general manager. Although from what I'd heard, she had the qualifications.

Generally known as Slobo, Krankovich was about five-six with a barrel chest and thick arms. A bald head that always seemed to be covered with fine beads of perspiration topped his huge shoulders. His shirt, usually unbuttoned to the middle of his chest, revealed large tufts of grayish brown hair and made him appear bear-like. A fanatically jealous man, he spent a great deal of time hanging around the station keeping an eye on his wife.

Not only was he jealous but also extremely combustible. I'd once seen him throw a salesman through a—fortunately open at the time—window because Slobo thought the poor guy had winked at Clarissa. Rumor had it that his money was loot gotten by questionable means during the breakup of Yugoslavia.

Travis had nicknamed him the Killer of Croatia, but even he was circumspect when actually around the man.

"I know Slobo didn't care for Travis," I said to Maggie. "But he doesn't like anyone."

"But you know Slobo. If he suspected Travis had given Clarissa even a lingering glance, he would get furious."

I could easily imagine Slobo hitting someone in a fit of anger, but murder was something else.

"But Clarissa must be at least ten years older than Travis."

Maggie grinned. "To Slobo, Clarissa is appealing to every man. It's really rather romantic when you think about it."

"Or would be if he wasn't a borderline psychopath. But do you think he could become furious enough to kill?"

"You know what they call him."

"Do you think that Killer of Croatia stuff is true?"

"There's enough of a possibility to make it worth checking out."

"I'll mention it to Malone and see what he thinks."

Maggie nodded. She reached out and gave me a hug.

"Don't worry, this will all work out for you eventually. Remember, orthoclase feldspar."

I smiled and actually did feel happier.

Chapter Thirteen

Malone pulled up in front of my house promptly at nine o'clock the next morning. I was all ready to check out Travis' apartment and hurried down the walk to meet him.

"Did everything go all right last night?" he asked as soon as I got in the car.

"Yep. There were no intruders, and I slept just fine."

That was a slightly modified version of the truth. I had triple checked every lock I could think of and had my softball bat next to me on the bed. But after a brief period of restlessness, I had fallen asleep and only awakened with the alarm.

Malone picked up a pile of papers between the two seats and tossed them in the back. One page that went by looked like an advertisement for a listening device.

"Office mail," he said.

"Do you get a lot of ads for different kinds of surveillance equipment?"

He nodded. "It's amazing how much high tech equipment is for sale now to make the life of the average private investigator easier and more effective— voice activated listening devices, long range video cameras, and computer programs for retrieving personal information. But sometimes the simplest stuff is best. When you're on a long stakeout a bottle with a good lid in invaluable because you're never close enough to a bathroom."

I grinned. "Do you ever buy any of these fancy gadgets?"

"Not very often. Along with the technology, you have to pay for a raft of courses and workshops on how to use it. I can't afford that or take the time away from work to learn how to utilize most of the technology. I usually get the essential equipment. I'm a pretty quick study, so I figure out how to use it on the job."

"Where are we heading?" I asked as Malone maneuvered us around the town green of Ridley.

"Just a few blocks more. I scoped it out yesterday afternoon. Travis lived in a small apartment building just outside the center of town."

We drove for another mile or so, and then Malone pulled up in front of Travis' building. It was plain looking but neat. There was a small front yard with several trees, and a sign pointing around the back for resident parking. We walked up to the front door, which gave us admittance to a small lobby. The inside door was locked, but next to one of the buzzers a label read *Superintendent*. Chance pushed the button and in response to an indistinct, tinny voice that gave a tentative "hello," Malone said that he wanted to ask a few questions about Travis Lambert. A couple of minutes later an older woman came down the hall to open the door.

"Are you with the police?" she asked suspiciously, keeping the door partway closed. She was wearing jeans with a bright floral blouse. Her short gray hair was attractively cut.

Malone held out his credentials and gave one of his

hundred-watt smiles. "I'm a private investigator working the Travis Lambert case."

The woman stared at him with a delighted expression.

"Are you really a private investigator?"

"Indeed, I am." He put out his hand. "I'm Chance Malone, and you are…?"

"Mrs. Margaret Tuttle."

"And this is a client of mine, Stormy McCloud."

She looked at me carefully. At first, I thought it was because of my unique name, but then she said, "Don't you broadcast the weather on television?"

"Yes."

Mrs. Tuttle looked at me as if I were a movie star, but she quickly turned her attention back to Malone.

"It's wonderful to meet you. You know, I love reading mysteries and watching them on television. Private eyes really fascinate me. I used to watch Perry Mason years back, but I guess he was a lawyer."

"I believe he was," Malone said.

"But I remember Sam Spade and Philip Marlow."

Malone nodded. "They led far more exciting lives than I do."

The woman winked at him. "Oh, I bet you have stories you could tell."

"Maybe a few, but I never tell them, of course, because everything I do is confidential," Malone said earnestly.

"Of course," the woman said, her wink replaced by a serious, slightly complicit expression. "How can I help you?"

"Well, I'm not sure you're going to be able to," Malone said, the disappointment clear in his voice. "But what I'd really like to do is take a look at Travis' apartment."

The woman frowned. "The police told me not to let anyone in the apartment without their permission. If I called them, would they say it was all right?"

"To be honest, they wouldn't, Margaret, if I may call you that?"

"Of course."

"You know how it is between the police and private investigators. The police are always afraid that we're going to show them up. It's very competitive."

"Oh, I can imagine." She paused and looked confused. "I'm just not sure how I can help."

"I realize that it's a difficult decision. But, you know, what the police are worried about is that someone will remove an item that will later turn out to be evidence. Now if I promise not to remove anything, and you stay with me while I go through the apartment, you would be able to say with a clear conscience if it should ever come up, which it probably never will, that I removed nothing from Travis' apartment. Would you be comfortable with letting me look around on those terms?"

The woman thought for a moment, then smiled.

"I don't see where anyone can have an objection to that. After all, if you do discover something, it would only help to solve the case. The police must want that as much as you do."

"That's certainly true."

She opened the door, inviting us both inside.

"And I expect that you want to find out what happened to your friend," she said to me.

It took a moment for it to click that she was

referring to Travis. When I realized what she meant, I quickly told her that was exactly why I was there.

"Travis' apartment is on the first floor. We just make a right and go to the end of the hall."

"Did you know him well?" Malone asked the woman as we walked down the hall.

"Not really. Some of the tenants I run into in the laundry room, and we chat a bit. But Travis worked mornings and early afternoons. I know because I'd see him on the news. I tried to ask him about his job the first few times I saw him, but he didn't seem to want to talk about it, at least not with me. Forgive me for saying it," she said, glancing back at me, "he was a nice-looking young man, but a bit stuck on himself if you catch my drift."

I nodded, trying not to agree too enthusiastically.

"Of course I can see how that can happen when you're on television. Even if you only broadcast the weather, you're a local celebrity, and people recognize you wherever you go. It must be easy to get a swelled head."

"It's something to guard against," I responded.

"I suppose being in the public eye must be very challenging."

"I wouldn't know," said Malone.

Margaret Tuttle grinned. "Neither would I."

She stopped in front of a door in the corner and fished a key out of her front jeans pocket.

"Master key," she said.

We stepped into Travis' apartment. You could see the whole place from the front door. There was a fair-sized living room with a sofa and an occasional chair, both positioned to provide a clear view of the large flat screen television, which seemed to be the only extravagance in the room. Behind the living room on the right was a doorway open to a bedroom. I could just make out the unmade bed. That made me think idly of something my mother used to say about always making your bed because you never knew what could happen to you during the day. That had certainly turned out to be true in Travis' case. To the left was a doorway into the kitchen. Part of the wall had been cut out so you could see from the kitchen counter into the living room. Although that had probably been done for reasons of style, all it did now was reveal a pile of dirty dishes.

Margaret put her hands on her hips and looked unhappy. "I don't care what the police say. If we don't get things cleaned up in here, we'll have vermin."

The sour smell of garbage reinforced that notion.

"I'm just going to take a look around," Malone said.

"I'm going to get some plastic bags, and get that garbage out of the kitchen," Mrs. Tuttle said. "You won't take anything while I'm gone, will you?"

"Of course not," Malone replied with a reassuring smile.

I followed Malone around as he examined the room. A quick glance revealed nothing other than the fact that Travis took both a local newspaper and one from Boston. He probably figured that being well informed was part of his job description, even if he did only report the weather. The drawer at one end of the sofa revealed nothing other than a set of coasters with pictures of national parks. In his bedroom, a small desk contained tax information and booklets on his health care and life insurance plans. Malone showed me his checkbook and the paperwork for several substantial money market accounts.

"I wonder how he managed to save all of this?" said Malone.

"He didn't. Not on his salary alone," I said. "Even if he lived very frugally, which we know he did not, he couldn't have put aside this much. Of course, maybe he had a lot of savings from the past."

Malone shook his head. "The dates when these were opened are within the last year. So it looks like Travis had a source of income other than predicting the weather."

Another odd thing about the apartment was the complete absence of any photographs of loved ones. A bit like mine, in that regard. There were several photos of Travis with famous television personalities, but none of family members or girlfriends. The whole place had a kind of recently-moved-into-it quality that was odd considering that Travis had lived there for a couple of years. Perhaps it wasn't so odd if you looked at it as a temporary way station on the road to greener pastures. That may have been Travis' hope. Picking a news magazine off the desk, Malone grunted in surprise when a birthday card fell out from among the pages. The envelope was blank, so clearly Travis had been planning to send it but had never gotten around to it. A brief note inside said—*I'll see that you have a Happy Birthday in Deming.*

"Where's Deming?" Malone asked.

"It's in New Mexico."

Malone raised an eyebrow.

"Weather people have to know their geography. But that's all I know about it."

"I'll check it out later on the computer and see if it gives me any ideas."

Margaret returned and started rummaging in the kitchen, so we used the opportunity to search the bathroom thoroughly, including the obvious spot inside the toilet tank. We found nothing. The bedroom closet revealed little beyond the fact that Travis had an extensive wardrobe of clothes for both business and leisure. A search through the dresser and nightstand was equally unrewarding. Short of tearing up the floorboards, there wasn't much else we could do.

Malone and I went out into the kitchen where Mrs. Tuttle was clearing the garbage from the table and putting it into a bag. I held the bag for her to make the job easier.

"Thank you, my dear." She glanced at Malone who was checking into canisters and looking behind the items stored on shelved. "Are you looking for something in particular?"

Malone smiled and shook his head. "Not really. I'm just trying to get a sense of the kind of guy he was. People tend to hide the things that tell you the most about themselves."

"Like drugs?

Chance and I both looked at Mrs. Tuttle in surprise. She laughed.

"I'm not really that clever. That's what the police said they were looking for when they searched the place. They asked me if I ever saw Travis using drugs or whether he had a lot of nighttime visitors. I had to tell them I didn't know. I don't spy on the tenants, and anyway, you can get to Travis' apartment without going past mine. Like I told you before, I hardly ever saw him. Mr. Macdonald, the owner of the building, knew him better. In fact, he'll probably be happy that Travis is no longer a tenant."

"McDonald. Would that be Bud McDonald?" I asked. I hadn't been aware that my landlord owned an entire apartment building.

"That's right," the woman replied, scraping some dishes into the garbage bag and filling the sink with sudsy water. "I'm going to wash these, and I don't care whether the police like it or not. If we get roaches in one apartment, before long they'll be in all of them. They can go through walls like they weren't there."

"I'll dry," I volunteered, taking a dishtowel off the rack.

"A television personality helping me with the dishes. I'll have to tell my friends about this."

We worked in companionable silence for a few moments; then I asked, "Why would Mr. McDonald be happy to get Travis out of here?"

"Well, Mr. McDonald said to me once that Travis was getting a special discount on his rent."

"Do you know why?" Malone asked, listening in on our conversation.

"When I asked him, Mr. McDonald said something about it being for old times' sake. I don't know what he meant, and I didn't feel free to ask. I wasn't implying that he had anything against Travis by what I said before. I just figured that Mr. McDonald would be happy now that he can charge the next tenant the full rate."

The three of us spent the next fifteen minutes setting things to rights in the apartment until finally, Mrs. Tuttle said, "Well, that will just have to do.

Anything else will have to wait until his next of kin remove his belongings." Suddenly she put a hand to her mouth and her eyes filled with tears. "Isn't it sad to think of a young man like that being dead?"

Malone put an arm around her shoulders.

"And not just dead," she said, "but murdered. Will you find out who did it?"

"I'll give it my best try," Malone said.

Ten minutes later, after more conversation with Margaret Tuttle, we left the building. As we went down the walk toward Malone's car, a black limousine pulled up behind it. A large man, who looked similar to our assailant from the other night, got out of the driver's side and quickly walked toward us. The man pulled back the flap of his jacket to show that he had a gun on his hip.

I gave Malone a sidelong glance to see how we were going to play this. He showed no signs of intending to put up a fight. That familiar sinking in the pit of my stomach was back, but I followed his lead.

"So you managed to get another weapon since last night," Malone said to the man.

"I've got a lot of guns." He patted Malone down. "You're not carrying my gun?"

"I gave it to the police."

"Yeah, sure."

Malone shrugged. "It's a good thing you've got a lot of them. But let's hope you didn't use that last one to commit any crimes."

The man opened the back door of the limo and gave Malone a shove, "Get in the car." He stood back and let me get in without the help of a push. What a gentleman.

Malone climbed in. I followed.

Across from us sat a slender man who appeared to be Indian or Pakistani. The man wore sunglasses, so it was impossible to read his eyes.

"Mr. Malone, it's a pleasure to meet you at last, and you as well, Ms. McCloud. Our paths seem to be crossing frequently in the course of this little venture," he said with the lilting English inflection that I associated with India.

"And you are?" Malone asked.

"My name doesn't really matter. You may call me Mr. Adams. My real name is considerably more complicated."

"Well, Mr. Adams, I wasn't aware that our investigation was being so closely watched," Chance said.

"Actually, you have proven to be something of an impediment to my search."

"I certainly didn't mean to be."

"My colleague in the front seat would disagree after the other night."

"He was trespassing on the property of Ms. McCloud, whom I am being paid to assist. We had a natural conflict of interest."

Mr. Adams smiled. "*Natural conflict of interest,* that's nicely expressed. I am hoping you will prove to be the kind of man with whom I can do business."

Malone shrugged. "That depends on the business."

"I am in what can loosely be called the import export business. As you may have guessed from my appearance and accent, most of my business is with the Indian subcontinent. Recently some items I imported to sell to some associates of mine went missing.

Unfortunately, the person responsible for bringing them into this country had a weakness for drugs of which I was unaware. He used my merchandise as collateral for a drug purchase, but then the dealer refused to sell my merchandise back to him at the agreed upon price."

"I'm sure that bothered you a great deal."

"Since the property was worth far more than the drugs, you could say I was very annoyed. The person who brought the merchandise into this country has learned a hard lesson."

"And so has the person who refused to sell the goods back to you, if that was Travis Lambert."

"It was indeed Mr. Lambert. But his demise had nothing to do with us. I agreed to buy my property back from him at a mutually agreed upon price. But Mr. Lambert never showed up to make the exchange, and shortly afterwards we found out he had been killed. As I am sure you realize, we would not have even considered killing him until our property had been returned, and if it had been returned, we would not be sitting here discussing this matter right now.

"So you think someone stole your property after killing Lambert?"

"That seems a reasonable supposition. Have you found my property?"

"I didn't kill Lambert."

"Well, perhaps Ms. McCloud has it then." The black lenses of the sunglasses turned toward me. Although I couldn't see his eyes, I imagined them to be a penetrating force. I felt he could see into my mind.

"I didn't kill Travis," I said in a voice that I hoped sounded both firm and honest.

"The police seem to think so."

"They're wrong."

"Perhaps. They often are."

"If you told us what the property was like, we could look for it along the way," Chance suggested.

The blank eyes turned to Malone, and I had the uncanny feeling the he already knew that we'd found the statue of Indra. I pushed the idea away as being unlikely.

"Let's just say they are Indian artworks, and you would know them if you found them."

"And you guessed they were in Ms. McCloud's backyard?"

Mr. Adams waved his hand casually. "We simply did not know where else to look. We have already searched Mr. Lambert's apartment, as have you, and found nothing. We thought that perhaps he had them on his person at the time of death, but my contacts within the police tell me they did not find them on his body. My colleague searched Ms. McCloud's property during the daylight hours today and found nothing, so, to use an Americanism, we are stumped. That's why we have turned to you."

I sent up at silent prayer of thanks that Malone had searched my yard shortly after dawn, another case of the early bird getting the Indra.

"We have no interest in your missing artworks. We're looking for the person who killed Travis Lambert so that Ms. McCloud won't be arrested for murder."

"But again, as I said before, our paths tend to overlap. Can you possibly doubt that the person who killed Lambert is also the person who stole my art works? And if we locate the one, we locate the other."

"That seems possible although not certain."

"I am willing to use it as my working hypothesis. And, in fact, I am willing to make you an offer based on the likelihood that my hypothesis is correct."

Malone held up a hand to stop him.

"I already have a job and a client. I can't be working on the same case for two people with possibly diverging interests."

"You misunderstand me. I wish you to discover who killed Mr. Lambert. If that involves vindicating Ms. McCloud, all the better. The important thing is that I be allowed to speak with the killer and insure that my property is returned to me before the law takes its course. Otherwise, it will be impounded as evidence and never returned to me, its rightful owner."

"And what if the police apprehend this individual before I do?"

Mr. Adams smiled. "From what I know of your reputation, I believe that is rather unlikely."

"But won't this person have to contact you anyway to sell the merchandise?"

Mr. Adams shook his head sadly. "There is always the possibility that they will find another avenue through which to make the sale. Then I will be excluded. I cannot allow that to happen."

"Assuming I do apprehend this thief before the police, what exactly am I looking for?"

"You are not looking for anything," Mr. Adams snapped. I could imagine his eyes flashing behind the glasses. "You notify me when you have a suspect, I will retrieve my property. Do you understand?" He handed Malone a business card.

Malone nodded. "And after that, I will be allowed

to turn this person over to the police?"

"Indeed. And you will be amply rewarded for your services to me."

I had a gut feeling that this little scenario would never come true. I doubted that somebody who stole from Adams would be allowed to live, and certainly not if he could tell the police about Mr. Adams' business. As far as our reward, we'd probably be lucky to get out of this alive.

Mr. Adams must have detected some hesitation on our part, because he went on, "If you choose not to take me up on my offer, I'm afraid that I will need to have a more *intense* conversation with Ms. McCloud to make certain that she is not the killer and does not know the whereabouts of my property. If you care about her in any way, I don't think you would want that to happen."

I could see Malone's mouth tighten, but he kept his anger in check. My chest constricted until it was difficult to breathe. Just being threatened was almost enough to kill me.

"If any harm should come to Ms. McCloud, there would be consequences," Chance said coldly.

Mr. Adams waved his hands as if sweeping away the implied threat.

"Let us avoid all this contentiousness. Accept my offer."

"It's a deal," Malone said softly.

Mr. Adams pushed a button on the armrest and a few seconds later the man with the gun opened the door.

"I hope the next time we meet will be under mutually beneficial circumstances," Mr. Adams said as we left the car.

Malone nodded to the man holding the door, who gave him a long, unfriendly look.

****

When we were back in Malone's car and driving away, he said, "Are you okay?"

"About as good as I ever feel after being threatened with torture."

"That's not going to happen."

"Are you really going to give him the killer?"

"I don't know what I'm going to do about that yet."

"You can't let them murder someone, even another murderer."

"We'll have to see how this plays out, okay?"

I nodded.

"At least we know a lot more than we did before. Lambert got the figurine from Adams' courier in exchange for drugs, then he bargained with Adams for more than the drugs were worth."

"But then someone other than Adams killed Travis, leaving the figurine behind."

"Maybe he or she just couldn't find it," Malone suggested.

"Or they didn't even know about it. Maybe the person killed Travis for some other reason."

"What?"

I shook my head.

"Well, we'd better find out soon before Mr. Adams and his friend become impatient."

That was an idea I could get behind.

Chapter Fourteen

All through the day, I kept wondering who could have killed Travis. I did my job on automatic pilot, and fortunately, no one seemed to notice. When I said good night to Maggie and Ray at the end of the eleven o'clock broadcast, I found that I hated to leave the brightly lit building for the dark walk across the parking lot. Mr. Adams' threat had spooked me, there was no getting around it. I pictured spending another night at home alone with all the lights on and baseball bat in hand. My rational mind told me that Mr. Adams wouldn't act until he was quite certain that Malone wasn't going to catch the killer. But my rational mind didn't do much for the feeling laying in the pit of my stomach as I headed along the road toward home.

But what else could I do? I really didn't want to ask Malone if I could spend another night in his office. That would make me look awfully weak, and I didn't relish spending the night at the one motel in town. I'd almost asked Maggie if I could stay with her, but although I considered Maggie a friend, she was such a private person that I was reluctant to impose on her. I was also hesitant to stay with any of my other friends because I didn't want to bring trouble to their doors. I could have asked Malone to sleep on my living room sofa, but again it would make me look weak, and it wasn't really fair to take advantage of his good nature if

I wanted our relationship to remain purely professional.

As I pulled the car into the driveway, I decided to make a dash for the front door. I might look foolish, but at eleven forty-five at night there was no one around to see. But as I ran up the walk, a figure suddenly arose in front of me. I gave a muffled scream and began to struggle as it put its arms around me.

"It's me Stormy. It's David."

The arms released me, and I stepped back. I stood there gasping for breath and in the light of the street lamp saw that it really was David Palmer.

"What are you trying to do, scare the life out of me?" I said when I was finally able to catch my breath.

"I'm so sorry that I frightened you. I tried to call, but I missed you at the office. And I don't have your cell phone number. I decided to just wait for you on the steps. I didn't intend to frighten you, but you came running up so suddenly I didn't have a chance to warn you."

"What are you doing here, anyway?"

"I have some more information about the statue you showed me, and I wanted to tell you about it right away."

It occurred to me that maybe I was being a bit unfair to David. After all, he didn't know that a man had been prowling around my house at night, or that a professional criminal had threatened me this morning. But still, showing up after eleven at night without a call was a bit odd.

"I know that coming this late must seem strange," he said as if he could read my mind, "But I'm tied up most mornings when you're free. And to be honest, I did want to see you again in person."

This last sentence was said in a warm, personal way. I found it was hard to remain angry with a man who said such nice things.

"Okay. Actually, I do stay up for a little while to unwind when I first get home. Why don't you come inside and tell me what you've found out."

I noticed that my hands still shook slightly as I put the key in the lock. I also made sure that the hall light was on for a couple of moments before I went inside.

"What a wonderful house," David said, as he followed me into the living room. You don't see many of these old arts and crafts style bungalows with any of the original features remaining."

"I know. The landlord did a good job with it. Maybe someday I'll be able to afford some mission style furniture to go along with it. What I have right now are just odds and ends I picked up at previous places I've lived."

"If you ever need any help, let me know. I've got some experience in interior design."

I nodded and motioned for him to sit on the sofa.

"Would you like something to drink?"

"A cup of tea would be nice."

I went out into the kitchen and put the kettle on to boil. I checked my phone messages and found nothing important. Deciding I didn't want anything for myself, I put a teabag in a cup and a few minutes later added the boiling water. When I returned to the living room, David was wandering around the first floor looking at what little there was to see. His curiosity reminded me a bit of Chance.

"Hope you don't mind my surveying the premises. You can often find out a lot about a person by seeing how they decorate."

"Not in my case," I said. "I just haven't had the time to get to it."

David didn't bother trying to deny that my place lacked class.

"Thank you," he said, taking the cup and returning to his place on the sofa. I sat in a chair across from him.

"So you have some information for me?" I asked.

David squirmed nervously on the sofa. "Actually I have a confession to make. I decided to investigate further into the background of your little statue. Although, as I said this morning, there are a lot of Indian items around not many are of the early gods and goddesses. Also, this one had a certain smell of authenticity."

"Smell?"

David smiled. "I don't mean that literally, although sometimes the sense of smell can tell you a lot. A canvas of a certain age has a special kind of aroma. But here I mean a kind of intuition. Any good curator develops a sense of when something is old and when it's been recently produced. Your statue is either very old or an excellent copy. Since I couldn't see any reason why someone would be copying statues of the ancient gods because there really isn't much of a market for them today, I figured it was likely to be an original."

"Go on."

"So I called a friend of mine who works for the Boston branch of the FBI. He checked with a friend of his in the fine arts division down in Washington, and it turns out that a set of ten statues of the ancient gods was recently stolen from a private collection in Mumbai,

India."

"You notified the FBI! How could you get us in trouble like that?"

David raised a calming hand. "Don't worry. I kept it all anonymous and vague. I said that a dealer I had met in passing had mentioned seeing the piece. Believe me, the FBI isn't going to bother following up on this. It wasn't stolen from a museum in this country, and these aren't famous masterpieces although they are quite valuable. My friend said that if I heard anything more concrete, I should let him know. I'm sure the whole thing will be filed away as a short note in their massive bureaucracy never to be seen again unless we pursue it."

I was still worried and let him know.

"You shouldn't have done this, not without discussing it with Malone and me first."

"You're absolutely right," he said, looking remorseful. "But I really didn't expect to find that the item was stolen. And this way, if you should ever have to turn in the statue to the police, you can claim that you did notify the FBI."

"I suppose."

"Also, you weren't fully honest with me," David added with a faint note of criticism in his voice. "If this is a piece of stolen goods, you didn't just happen to come across it. Is this linked in any way to the death of Travis Lambert?"

"Why should it be?"

"It stands to reason. You find his dead body on your property and the next day come to see me with the statue and a private investigator in tow. Only a fool would think the two are unconnected."

"I honestly don't know with certainty if they are related." I took a deep breath and told him about Malone finding the statue at the murder scene. "But whether it had anything to do with the murder or not, we have no idea. That statue could have been out there for months."

"No, the theft only occurred last week."

"Well, I doubt that Travis was the thief. He certainly didn't go to India last week." I wasn't about to tell David about Mr. Adams.

"He could have been the go-between."

"I suppose."

"And you only found the one piece? There are supposed to be ten."

"We only found one."

"Are you sure?"

"Are you accusing me of being a liar?"

"Of course not, but Malone was the one who found it."

"Malone is no liar either," I said. The idea was absurd. He was probably the most honest man I knew. I paused for a moment, wondering why I was so afraid of getting involved with him if I really did think he was so honest.

"Very well," David said. He sat sipping his tea and looking across the room for a long moment. "The god Indra is really quite interesting. As I said, he is the god of war and storms. But he was also commonly associated with a hallucinogenic drug used during the ancient religious festivals called soma."

I smiled to myself at the irony that Travis, who had used and sold drugs, had ended up associated with a deity involved with them as well.

"What do you think we should do with the statue?" I asked.

"You could take it to the police. Of course, they'll be angry at you for withholding evidence. A better plan might be to give it to me, and I could turn it over to my friend at the FBI. There'd be no questions asked, and given the way the FBI communicate with the locals, the Ridley police would probably never find out about it."

"I'll have to talk it over with Malone."

"Fine, but remember he should be working for you. So whatever he does must be in your best interest."

"I'm sure it is."

Just then the phone rang, and I answered. It was Malone.

"I just called to check to see if you were all right alone in the house."

"Well, I'm not exactly alone. David is here with me."

"Oh."

"He stopped by to tell me more about the statue."

"I'd like to go to the station tomorrow morning and talk to the day shift. They were the people who actually worked with Travis. Maybe they'll be able to tell me something new. I figured you'd like to go with me."

"I definitely would."

"How about I pick you up around nine again and drive you in to the station."

"I'm having lunch with my friend Gloria tomorrow, so I'll need my car."

"I'll take you back home after we're done so you can get your car," Malone said.

"Sounds fine." I wondered if he was staying close to me because of Mr. Adams. Anyway, I wasn't going to turn down the offer of protection.

"And don't be telling David anything that he doesn't need to know."

"I won't," I said, knowing that I already had.

"I'm really looking forward to our date on Sunday," David said, showing no signs of leaving after I hung up the phone.

"So am I. But right now I have to ask you to go because I really need my beauty sleep," I said, standing and heading down the hall.

"Of course, of course." David scrambled off the sofa and followed me. At the door, he gave me a vigorous hug and a kiss on the cheek. "Remember, if you need my help with that statue, don't be afraid to ask. I'm sure I can work things out so you don't get in any trouble."

"Thanks for your help," I said, as I closed the door behind him.

Chapter Fifteen

The next morning Malone and I set out together for the television station. We'd been driving along for about five minutes when I noticed that he seemed to be glancing frequently in his rear view mirror.

"What do you see?" I finally asked.

"Nothing for sure, but I've got a feeling that we're being followed. The same dark sedan has been staying two cars back for the past ten minutes."

"Are your feelings usually right?"

"It's always good to pay attention to them because it could be your unconscious mind trying to tell you something that might keep you alive. In Afghanistan when a little voice told you that there was an ambush up ahead, even if you couldn't have said what you'd actually seen or heard that tipped you off, it was usually a good idea to take that voice seriously."

"How do you think they found us?"

"The tail was probably waiting outside my office and picked me up there. I'll bet it's someone working for Mr. Adams who's just making sure that I'm on the case and trying to keep a record of the people I'm talking to."

"Can we lose him?"

"Sure, I know all the streets and back alleys in Ridley, but what's the point. It isn't like we're going anywhere secret."

Malone drove sedately to the studio. When we parked in the lot, we watched as the other car went past the building and around the bend in the road.

"Since this studio is in such a remote spot, our tail is going to have a tough time finding an inconspicuous place to wait. We'll probably spot him when we leave."

As we walked into the lobby, Mia looked up with an exuberant smile. She was wearing a blue blouse that accentuated her eyes, and she certainly seemed happier than the last time we'd spoken with her. Apparently at least one person had benefited from Travis' demise.

Malone gave her one of his usual dazzling smiles. "You're looking particularly happy and pretty today."

"Thanks. And I am happy. I just heard from Clarissa that they're going to try me out for an on-air spot tomorrow. They're having an outdoor food festival downtown, and I'm going to be the one to cover it."

We both congratulated her.

"What do you have to do?" I asked.

"Eat and ask the vendors what's in their food." She frowned. "I know it isn't like doing hard news, but it will help me develop my on-air personality."

"I'm sure it will," Malone said. "And who knows what you'll be doing next."

"Probably more soft news. Hildie has a lock on the out of studio hard news coverage, and she's not the type to share. I heard that Clarissa had to really fight to get Hildie to let me do this much. She sees everyone who's out in the field in front of a camera as a threat to her."

"Clarissa must have thought you were ready, to go to bat for you like that," I said.

"I suppose. But the other thing is that Hildie has offended so many people in the community with her hard-nosed approach that they don't even want to talk to her. The other stations get the scoop on us because folks are afraid to be interviewed by her."

"Yeah. She even tried to get me to confess on camera to being a murderer," I said.

Mia nodded. "When Mr. Harris heard about that, I think it was the last straw. He probably would have fired Hildie that day, but Clarissa pointed out that we had no one to replace her. I guess that's why I'm getting my chance."

"Good luck at getting your shot to replace her," said Malone.

"She might try to bump me off first." Mia covered her mouth and made wide eyes. "I guess I shouldn't joke about that under the circumstances."

Malone grinned. "I think you're pretty safe. The worst Hildie probably gets is obnoxious."

Mia leaned across the counter toward us. "I wouldn't be too sure of that," she whispered.

"What do you mean?" I asked.

"Well, a while back Hildie got this idea that she wanted to do crime features. She even tried to blackmail poor Ray into helping her."

"Helping her how?" Malone asked.

"By letting himself be filmed making a drug buy in downtown Springfield. She promised to hide his identity but insisted that she needed to photograph a real buy to use as a lead-in to the story. She said it would give the spot credibility."

"What did Ray say?" I asked.

"He went crazy. He told her she was nuts if she thought he was going to commit a crime on camera. But she kept after him. She even threatened to tell Mr.

Harris that she saw Ray smoking pot outside the studio several times. Ray denies that he ever smokes at work, but, you know, the way he looks Mr. Harris might have believed her."

"What did Ray do?" I asked.

"He told Hildie she should talk to Travis, that he was much better connected with the drug scene. And that since Travis was interested in getting into doing the news, maybe he'd take her up on it."

"Travis wanted to switch from meteorology?" I asked.

Mia shrugged. "There was a rumor that he'd had a tape done with him working as anchorperson. Maggie supposedly helped him set it up. He thought that was the way he'd get into a bigger market. Travis was never satisfied with what he had."

"So what happened when Hildie asked him to help her?" asked Malone.

"I don't know. She doesn't talk to anyone much, other than her cameraman, Sam. It's like they're a team, and the rest of us are outsiders. But I don't think she would have killed Travis for not helping her. She isn't that vicious."

"Well, that's good to know," Malone said dryly.

After saying goodbye to Mia, we walked past the counter and down the hall. As we passed Clarissa Hayes' office, she stepped out.

"Can I talk to the two of you for a moment?" she asked, motioning us inside. She carefully closed the door and turned to face us.

"Have you been making any progress on the case?"

"Some," Malone said. "But it's still quite early."

Clarissa tugged gently on her shoulder length hair,

then rested a hip against the edge of the desk.

"Look, I know Simon said that you should find the truth and let the chips fall where they may, but he doesn't have to run this station on a day-to-day basis. I know some people who work here aren't angels, it appears that Travis certainly wasn't but I'd rather that you didn't go running to the police with every detail you discover."

"I wouldn't dream of it. My job is to find out what happened to Travis Lambert. If it isn't related to that, then I have no intention of going to the police. And I wouldn't inform the police without telling you and Mr. Harris first."

"Okay," she said, relaxing. "I guess we'll just have to see what happens."

"Yes, I guess we will."

"What was that all about?" Chance asked as we walked down the hall to the bullpen.

"I'm not sure. Could be there's something she hoped wouldn't get out?"

Chance nodded, looking thoughtful.

"There's the morning broadcast team," I said, pointing to a man and woman standing in one of the cubicles. "That's Joan Carmichael and Roger Ziemba."

We walked over, and I introduced Chance to the two of them. Joan, who asked to be called Joanie, was a young woman with short blonde hair, while Roger, as handsome as she was cute, had long wavy hair. There was a sameness that made them look like brother and sister.

"So you folks do an early morning broadcast?" Malone asked.

Roger nodded. "We do a five-thirty and a six-thirty. Then we do morning updates, and another half hour at noon. Holly and Debbie take over after that."

"And Travis was the weatherman who worked with you?"

"Most of the time," Joanie said. "Except on weekends. If we had to cover on a weekend, we worked with Brian Croaker."

"What was it like to work with Travis?" Malone asked.

The two anchor people looked at each other as if trying to decide who would begin.

"We really didn't have much to do with him," Roger finally said. "He'd come in, get his report ready, and give it in a professional way. Then he'd keep to himself the rest of the time. He wasn't the kind of guy who would hang out with you in the break room."

"Not unless he had something flashy to tell you about, like his newest car or recent trip to the islands. He was a great one for bragging," Joanie said.

"And he was always busy," Roger added. "Always on his cell phone taking calls."

"One thing has been bothering me. Travis was the senior weather person, right?" Chance asked.

"And he never let me forget it," I added.

"He was here a year and a half or so before Stormy," Joan said. "He came about a year after I did."

"So isn't it customary for the senior weatherman to be on during the evening shift? That's the way it is on other stations, am I right?"

Joan nodded. "When the guy who was senior to Travis quit, they offered him the night slot, but he didn't want it. So when they hired Stormy, they gave it to her. I know Travis passed up a pay increase to stay on days, but he said something about not wanting to work nights because it would mess up his sleep cycle. It didn't really make much sense to me."

"He always made a big deal of telling Stormy that he was the senior weather person, but in reality, she was doing the job," Roger said, smiling at me. "Travis seemed to resent her popularity, but at the same time, he refused to give up the day shift where there are fewer viewers. I know that I'd give it up in a second to get on the evening broadcast. It's a much better stepping stone to a larger market."

"So why do you think Travis really wanted days?" Malone asked.

Joanie and Roger glanced at each other again as though they were communicating telepathically. Finally, Roger said, "We don't know for sure. All we can say is that Travis seemed to have some kind of business going on the side. When we did happen to overhear his phone calls, they were often about the prices for something."

"Can you be more specific?"

"Not really," Roger said.

"There's a rumor going around the Travis was dealing drugs. Could the calls have been related to that?"

Roger shrugged. "They could have been."

After thanking the two anchor people, we went across the room, and I introduced Malone to Brian Croaker. The man had a wonderfully deep, rich voice like the old radio announcers, but unfortunately, he couldn't tell us much about Travis.

"Sure. I used to see him around once in a while, but he pretty much ignored me." Brian gave a deep, throaty chuckle. "I think he figured he was too good for me because I was only a retired fill-in. Of course, I've probably done more in my career in radio and television than he'd ever have accomplished, even if he had lived to a ripe old age."

"Lack of talent?" Malone asked.

"He had adequate talent. It was his bad attitude. He was only out for himself, and it was obvious to everyone. People like that never get very far in this business. You have to be ambitious, of course, but you have to soften it a little by being nice to other people. After all, you work as a team, and if you aren't liked, your co-workers can make you look bad."

"Is that Travis' desk you're sitting at?"

"Yep. He never let me sit at it when he was alive. I always had to use Stormy's. Something about people messing with his stuff, although I never saw that he kept much around."

"Do you mind if I look inside the desk?" asked Malone.

"Help yourself," the big man said, rolling out of the way on his desk chair.

Malone pulled open the top drawer.

"Travis always kept it locked," I added. "I guess the police left it open the other day after they searched it."

We quickly went through the drawers but found nothing other than office supplies, a few station policy bulletins, and a handful of local maps.

"Nothing much there, right?" Croaker asked.

"Not that I can see," Malone replied.

"Yeah, he never kept anything personal around here as far as I could tell. He was a boy who played his cards close to his chest."

Malone nodded. "Do you think he had a lot of cards to play?"

"By the smug look on his face all the time, I'd say that he thought so."

"Who are the producer and the cameraman on the day shift?" Malone asked me.

"Jack Stephano is the producer/director and Lonny Canfield works the camera. They're both in the studio now," I said.

We thanked Brian and headed across the hall. Opening the thick soundproofed studio door, the first person we saw was Jack Stephano, a thin guy with bulging eyes. At the moment he was pawing frantically through a pile of papers.

"What do you want?" he said to us without looking up.

"I'm Chance Malone. I'm investigating the murder of Travis Lambert."

"Yeah, I heard about you," he said, ignoring Malone's offered hand.

I felt thankful, as I often did, that I worked with Maggie and not with Jack, who was known for being disorganized and rude. Not a good combination for a producer/director, where discipline and orderliness are primary requirements.

"What can you tell me about Lambert?" Malone asked in a rougher voice.

"He did his job."

We waited, but nothing more was forthcoming.

"Anything else?" Malone prompted.

Stephano snatched a sheet of paper out of the pile. He smiled in relief and turned to face us.

"Like I said, he did his job. We weren't buddies. I didn't ask about his life outside of work, and he didn't ask about mine."

"How was he as a weather announcer?" Malone asked.

"Not the best I've seen, but by no means the worst. He spoke clearly and seemed confident on camera. That's all I ask."

"Did he have any enemies?"

"I'm sure he did. Everyone in the business does. It's a breeding ground for envy. Everyone wants what you've got, and once they have it, they want more."

"Any names?" Malone asked.

"It's usually the person right behind you in the pecking order who is out to get you. I guess in this case it would be you," Jack said, looking directly at me.

"I didn't have anything to do with Travis' death."

Jack shrugged as if such a denial was so predictable as to be boring.

"All I'm saying is that if you don't get arrested for his murder, you'll probably get to be senior meteorologist. You're the one with the most to gain."

Good old Jack, blunt and to the point.

"Did he have any particular enemies?"

"He could have had a hundred enemies outside work. I have no idea."

A younger man in a t-shirt strolled into the studio.

"What did you think of Lambert?" Stephano called out.

The kid shrugged. "He only wanted to be shot from his good side, just like all the rest of them. Otherwise, I didn't have much to do with him."

"Is there anyone here who would know more about

him?"

"I heard he was going out with Debbie on the nightly news. She could probably tell you a lot more about him," Lonnie said with a wink.

We thanked them for their help. I grabbed my coat, and we walked down the hall to the entrance, I filled Malone in on my conversation yesterday with Debbie.

"Not much new there," Malone said.

I nodded. "She was so much in love with him that she wouldn't have noticed if he sold drugs right in front of her."

Malone said goodbye to Mia, who still looked exhilarated at the new career opening up to her. We walked to the glass front door and looked down the road. I could see a car parked a hundred yards away with a direct sightline on the parking lot.

"Think he'll follow you or me when I get home?" I asked.

"I'm the one they expect to find the killer, so I'd say he'll stick with me. But we'll soon find out. If he does follow you, I'll have to have a talk with him."

We walked across the parking lot and got in Chance's car. As we drove away, Chance told me our tail was dutifully following us.

"What in the world was Travis thinking, trying to extort money from a man like Adams?" I asked.

"Like I told Mr. Harris, Travis had the prime characteristic of most arrogant people, he was a risk-taker. He thought he was so much smarter than everyone else that he could do just about anything and get away with it."

"But you don't think Adams killed Travis?"

"I don't think so. Like he said, he wouldn't have

killed him until he had the statue. And if he had the statue, he wouldn't be trying to make a deal with me."

"Statues. There's more than one."

"How do you know?"

"I'll tell you in a minute. So you believe Adams' story."

"If Adams or his thug had killed Travis they'd have taken their *statues* and been long gone. So I believe Adams' story that they were supposed to meet with Travis on the night he was murdered, but he never showed up."

"Because someone else killed him."

"Exactly."

"So we now know that Travis was an active drug dealer who decided to get involved with stolen art?" I asked.

"That's why he didn't want to work nights. It would have interfered with his drug dealing." Malone stopped and stared hard at me. "Now it's time for you to come clean and tell me how you know there is more than one statue."

I sighed. I hoped that Malone wouldn't be too angry or disappointed in me.

"You know that David came over last night?"

Malone's lips tightened, but he just nodded.

"Well, he got in touch with the FBI."

"The FBI! Over what?"

"The statue we showed him."

I could see the muscle bulging in his jaw and knew that he was controlling himself. He looked out at the road in front of him for a long moment. He was probably thinking that I was responsible for bringing David on board and that he had proved to be an unreliable ally.

"I'm sorry," I said. "I know this is entirely my fault. I never would have guessed that David would do this without asking our permission."

Malone forced a smile on his face. "Let's not panic until we see what damage has been done. What did he learn from the FBI, and how did they respond?"

"An agent in the field of art theft told David that a set of ten ancient Indian god statues had been stolen last week. Those must be Adams' merchandise."

"Is the FBI sending someone out here to investigate the theft?"

"Apparently not. David was pretty vague when he talked to them about where he had heard about the statue, and they just asked him to keep them informed if he learned any more about the items. David thinks that because it wasn't a theft in this country and the statues aren't famous, the FBI is probably not going to put much in the way of resources into finding them."

"Let's hope he's right."

"I'm afraid that what I did was even worse than that," I said, trying to look contrite. "I also told David where we found the statue."

"But he didn't say anything about that to the FBI?"

"He didn't know when he talked to them. And he's promised not to contact them again without our permission."

"I hope he does keep it to himself. If Green got wind of it, we'd be in a lot of trouble for withholding evidence."

"Don't worry. If that happens, I'll just tell Green it was all my idea."

"That won't matter. He'll blame me as the

professional who should have given you better advice. My license could be in jeopardy."

"I never should have insisted that we hide the statue from the police."

Malone reached out and put a hand on my shoulder. "Green doesn't know about it yet, so let's not worry about what hasn't happened."

"David offered to turn the statue over to the FBI for us, no questions asked. He thinks they might not even tell the Ridley police about it."

"He could be right. But until we have a better idea on how things are going to develop, I think we should hold onto it."

"On another topic, Maggie had a suggestion. She mentioned that Clarissa Hayes' husband, Slobodan Krankovich, didn't care for Travis."

"Ah, a new player and yet another person who didn't like Travis. Why not?"

"He's a very jealous man, and he suspected Travis of taking an undue interest in his wife."

"In Clarissa? She's an attractive woman, but she must be at least fifteen years older than Travis."

"I told you he was very jealous."

"How can I get in touch with him?

"He's a minority owner in the station and spends most afternoons in a small office he has next to his wife."

"Did he have any reason to suspect Travis of fooling around with Clarissa?"

"No, but that wouldn't stop him."

I described Krankovich's previous violent behavior and mentioned his nickname.

"The Killer of Croatia," Malone repeated with a

smile. "Is that for real?"

"That's what Travis used to call him, and it stuck."

Malone laughed. "The name alone might be enough for this guy to want to kill Travis. I think I'll have a talk with him this afternoon."

"Be careful," I warned. "He's pretty volatile."

"I'll be careful around anyone with a nickname like that. I wonder if he's the reason Clarissa is so concerned with what my investigation might reveal. Maybe she thinks her husband did something to Travis."

"Possibly."

"Well, have a good lunch with your friend."

"Thanks."

Malone looked like he was going to say more but then changed his mind. I got out of the car and went up to my front door. I looked up the block and saw our tail parked under a tree. Chance pulled away, and sure enough, the car that was under the tree took off right after him.

Chapter Sixteen

I drove down the mountain and over the secondary roads until I rolled into the center of Ridley, which had the standard New England town green with a Congregational Church and a variety of small shops and businesses surrounding it. Once this had been the economic center of town where everyone came to shop, but the construction of a mall two decades ago had changed the green into a haven for real estate offices, antique shops, and small restaurants. I learned from a story the station had done a few months ago that Benjamin Ridley, a blacksmith, and gun maker, who was an early settler in the area, had founded the town. I wondered, as I navigated the tight traffic around the green and pulled into public parking, what he would think of the place today.

I walked into the Lunch Wagon and stifled a yawn. I had slept better than expected but was still tired. I saw Gloria sitting by the wall talking on her cell phone. Waving off the hostess, I walked across the room toward my friend. Although its name suggested casual dining, part of the Wagon's charm was that it went against expectations. The tables boasted starched tablecloths, the floors were highly polished oak and the waitresses dressed in neat black uniforms.

Gloria got off the phone just as I joined her. She stood up and gave me a long hug. The cell phone rang, and she shut it off.

"That thing's been driving me crazy," Gloria said, making a face.

"So the real estate market has really bounced back?"

"It's starting to. I also went away for a long weekend at the end of last week, and it seems as if everybody picked that time to decide to buy or to list their house."

"Where did you go?"

"To a little inn on the Cape. Remember that guy Nick I mentioned meeting at an Open House about six weeks ago?"

"Sure. The last time we talked you'd gone out with him a couple of times and weren't sure it was going to lead to anything."

"I know. Nick isn't the kind of guy who exactly sweeps you off your feet. He's more like a steady drip of water that wears you down."

"Sounds painful," I said with a grin.

"Not really. It's just that every time I go out with him I find myself liking him just a little bit more. Until eventually I agreed to go away with him for the weekend. I know that's risky. Being alone together for all that time can either break or make a relationship."

"So which was it?"

Gloria took a deep breath, and her face went rosy.

"I think I'm in love."

I tried not to look too skeptical.

"You've thought that before. Many times, in fact."

"I know. But those times I was swept off my feet, and once I got over the initial rush of endorphins, I knew I'd made a mistake. This time, it's all happened so gradually that I think it might be real. I hope so, anyway. But I'm going to take lot of time before we move to the next step."

"You mean an engagement."

"I was thinking of living together a while first."

"Well, that's great news. I hope that things keep on going well for the two of you."

Suddenly the smile disappeared from Gloria's face.

"Here I am telling you all about my good news when you're the one who needs to talk. Have they made any more progress in finding out who killed Travis Lambert?"

The waitress came and gave us menus. We both chose the seafood salad, which was our favorite. When the waitress was out of earshot, I filled Gloria in on what had happened in the investigation so far.

"Sounds like the problem is that you can't explain why Travis died on your property," said Gloria.

"I have no idea why he was there. I didn't think he even knew where I lived."

"Does this private investigator have any ideas?"

"We've been working together, so I know as much as he does. All we can say with certainty so far is that Travis was a drug dealer trying to make it as an art thief."

"You're working together?"

"A condition of his employment."

"What's the matter?" Gloria asked. "Didn't you think the guy could do the job on his own?"

"It's not that. Well, maybe it was at first, but not anymore."

"I think you're blushing." Gloria looked at me more closely. "Yes, you are definitely blushing. So this has suddenly gotten a whole lot more personal. Is this private detective by any chance a handsome, virile kind of guy?"

"I guess you could say that."

I didn't reveal any more. Even with my female friends, I find it hard to talk about my feelings. Like my father, I tend to keep them inside and only express them in the form of logical ideas.

"So you met a handsome, charming guy, and you're sticking close to him. What's the problem in that?"

My logical mind kicked in. "Well, first of all, he's a private detective. What kind of job is that for a man? Do you even know any private detectives? How healthy can it be, always digging into people's lives? Can anyone even make any real money at it? What does your friend Nick do?"

"He's a contractor."

"See, there's a normal, salt of the earth kind of job."

"But he has up and down times depending on the economy. I do, too. Every job has its risks."

"Well, there's more. He's religious."

"You mean like in spending all his free time in church religious?"

"I don't know. I don't think so. But he reads the Bible, so I bet he goes to church pretty often."

"Honey, lots of people go to church. Even I go once in a while. Don't you believe in God?"

I stopped short, stumped by the simple question. "I don't know. I never thought about it much when I was growing up. It wasn't so much that I didn't believe as that I didn't really have religion as part of my life."

"Is this your father's influence again?" Gloria said. "You know I'm always telling you that you've got to live your own life."

"I know. I know."

"Do you think this guy Chance would try to force you to go to church?"

"I don't think he would *force* me to do anything. But if I didn't, I think there would always be a gulf between us. And what if we had children?"

"Aren't you getting a bit ahead of yourself? You haven't even gone out on a date with this guy yet."

"I like to have a plan. Just like in chess, I want to know what I'm going to do a few moves ahead."

"Love isn't chess. You can't predict what the outcome of each move is going to be. You make your move and see what happens, then you base you next move on that. You've got to be more flexible. After going out with this guy a couple of times, you may realize that this whole religion thing isn't going to be a problem at all."

"Or that it is, and I don't want to see him again," I said grimly.

"That's always possible. I'm not guaranteeing you won't get hurt. I'm just saying that you have to get involved in order to find out what's going to happen. You can't stand back and predict it like the weather."

"I guess I could go out with Chance once and see what happens."

"Sure. One date doesn't make a marriage. And on the children thing, you could always give them some training on both sides then let them decide for themselves."

"That didn't work very well with me," I said. I

went on to explain to Gloria how my father had given up on that plan once my mother left him.

"Just because it didn't work for you because of how deeply your father was hurt by your mother, doesn't mean you couldn't work it out for your children."

"I suppose. At least I would be there for them. I wouldn't abandon them."

Gloria paused while the waitress put our salads down in front of us. Even after the waitress went away, she sat quietly as if unsure whether to speak.

"You know, I understand why you've always judged your mother so harshly. Leaving her husband and daughter for another man is a terrible thing to do. But you've never heard her side of things. Maybe you should hold off on assigning blame until you do."

"You mean maybe she was crazy in love with this handsome, virile guy. You can see why falling in love makes me so nervous. How do I know I won't make the same mistake that my mother made?"

"It doesn't always turn out badly. You can't assume that you're just like your mother."

"I may get to find out what my mother is like," I said and repeated what my father had told me about getting in touch with her. "Who knows where that might lead?"

"After almost twenty years, he's going to give it another go?" Gloria said in amazement.

I smiled slightly. "I know. It's hard to believe. Do you think I should have him checked out for dementia?"

"There's nothing unhealthy about getting over your bitterness."

"He may have gotten over his, but I'm not sure I've gotten over mine. I don't know how to get over being cut out of her life like that. After she broke up with that guy, she could at least have come back to see me sometimes."

"Like I said, wait until you have all the facts."

I sighed. "None of this will matter if I end up in jail."

Gloria reached across the table and took my hand.

"Don't give up. This will work out. I'll be praying for you."

I gave her a small smile.

Chapter Seventeen

Back from lunch, I walked across the bullpen to where Chance was standing next to Brian Croaker. Chance's face lit up when I entered the room. He seemed absolutely delighted to see me, which made it even harder for me to sort out my confused feelings about him.

"How was your lunch?" Chance asked.

I shrugged. "Okay. As usual, I ate more than I should have."

"Yeah, you have to be careful. I've heard television adds ten pounds."

"Tell me about it," Brian Croaker said with a smile, patting his large waist.

"Did you want to talk to me?" I asked Chance.

"If you have the time."

"I've got a half hour until I have to work on my update. Let's go in the break room where we can talk."

Chance said goodbye to Brian and followed me across the room. He got an orange soda out of the machine.

"Do you want anything?" he asked.

I shook my head. "So what did you want to talk about?"

"I think we should question this Krankovich fellow this afternoon."

I nodded. "How about right after my update?"

"Good. You remember Mrs. Tuttle mentioning that Travis was getting a discount from your landlord, Bud Macdonald."

"Sure."

"I think I should have a chat with him this afternoon and find out exactly how well he knew Travis."

"Why don't you let me do that? I can get an hour off after my update. Bud knows me, and I can always pretend that I'm trying to find out when the work on my garage is going to resume."

"Sounds good."

I sighed and sank back in the chair.

"What's wrong?"

"Just feeling a little down."

"That's no surprise, considering."

Chance looked around him, surveying the break room.

"Are you happy being here?"

"In the break room?"

Chance laughed. "No, I mean in broadcasting."

"Overall, I enjoy it. Sometimes it seems cut-and-dried, basically just reporting what I get from the computers. Most of the time it doesn't take a lot of creativity or intelligence."

"Do you like being a 'personality'?"

"Not at all. I'm a shy person. I dread going out in public and having people recognize me. Most of the time, I wear a hat or pull a hood over my face, so I'll look different."

"Sounds tough."

"No, it sounds silly. I'm just a local celebrity. Take me fifty miles from Springfield, outside of our viewing area, and no one would know me."

"So why do you do television weather?"

"People really depend on me to give them an accurate weather forecast. I do my best to compare all the computer models and give them what, in my opinion, is the most accurate prediction I can. That's especially important in bad winter weather of which we get plenty."

"Any other reasons you stay with it?"

"Shear stubbornness. I want to prove something to my father."

"That's right. You mentioned that he didn't want you to be a meteorologist. He wanted you to be a college teacher."

"You were paying attention."

He smiled. "Being a good listener is important to a private investigator. But you've already become a success in your field. What else do you have to prove to him?"

"That I really am a success. I moved back here partly because he lives nearby. So he knows every night I'm going to be on television. Of course, he probably just watches another station, but deep down he must be aware that I'm on the air."

"Aren't you letting your anger toward him determine your life? By moving back here because of him, aren't you giving him control over you?"

"Everybody is influenced by something from their past. What about you? You wouldn't even tell me why you became a detective. With all you know about me, don't you think the time has come to share a little?"

Chance looked down at the institutional tiles on the floor. "I was in Afghanistan. As with most things, there were good times and bad."

"I'm sure there was more to it than that," I said.

Chance shrugged. "I came home and hooked up with a guy who had been over there with the MPs. He started a detective agency and hired a lot of veterans. I worked with him until I got my credentials."

"Your passion for the truth. Does that have anything to do with Afghanistan?"

"You'd make a pretty good detective yourself. You know that?" he said, giving me a sideways glance. "Actually my passion for the truth, as you call it, started before Afghanistan. I suppose it was part of me from my earliest upbringing. And one thing I'd been taught is that telling the truth sometimes costs. To make a long story short, my unit got caught in an ambush and some people died. There was an inquiry into what had happened, and everyone lied to protect our commanding officer, who had divided our force even though he knew the enemy was nearby, which is something you're never supposed to do."

"But you told the truth."

He nodded. "And since I was a lieutenant, it carried some weight, and our captain got a reprimand. I knew what I had done would get around, and I'd never receive another promotion. So I decided not to reenlist after my tour was up. I'd considered going career army, so that was a big decision for me."

"And couldn't you have bent the truth a little under the circumstances?"

"Once you start bending the truth, there's no telling where you'll stop. Pretty soon the truth is a pretzel that bears no relationship to reality."

"But you lied to Adams about being willing to

work for him, didn't you?"

Chance clenched his hands together. "Sometimes you have to lie where you're dealing with unscrupulous people. Or when it's necessary to accomplish something important."

"Like proving I didn't kill Travis. You lied to protect me."

"But it should never come easy, and it should never be done just to help yourself."

"I know the truth is important. I've been burned more than once by being on the receiving end of lies. There was Rick, this guy I went with in college. We were practically engaged. I don't know why I didn't see him for what he was. But he was Mr. Popularity, and I guess I liked going along for the ride.

"Then in our senior year, I suddenly started to see him less. He told me he was busy with some organization or the other, and, of course, I believed him. Then I started seeing him going around campus with other girls. When I confronted him, he at first claimed that they were friends he was just working with in some club, but people talk on a small campus. Before long I learned he'd been cheating on me and had been for quite a while."

Chance nodded. "Being betrayed like that is painful. But not all men are like this Rick."

He gently reached over and touched the back of my hand, and I thought how odd this conversation had been. I had told Chance something I'd never shared except with a few close girlfriends.

"No, some of them are like Slobo and intensely jealous. I'm not sure which is worse," I said, drawing my hand away.

"You know, before I talk to Slobo, I'd like to have a brief conversation with Ray. I'd like to find out if Travis took Hildie up on her offer to do a drug deal on camera. That could have something to do with his murder."

"Why don't we go over there right now and question Ray after my spot. Later on today, I'll have a chat with Hildie."

"Okay."

"And like I said, I'll also go see Bud MacDonald. I'm really curious to find out what type of relationship he had with Travis."

"Be careful. We don't know if there was something criminal going on."

"And you be gentle with Ray. He may be a bit of a flake, but he's no killer."

Chapter Eighteen

"Why did Hildie ask for your help with the drug documentary?" Chance asked.

"Aww, dude, I expected better of you," Ray groaned. As usual, he was wearing a faded t-shirt. This one said *Born Color Blind* across the front. His jeans were ripped in a way that I knew was fashionable in some quarters.

Chance leaned against the counter in the break room, and I stood in the doorway to keep others out. We'd guessed we'd find Ray there right after I finished the mid-afternoon weather spot. Whenever he wasn't behind the camera, he seemed to head directly for the coffee. He was holding a cup of brew under his nose right now as if the aroma would drive away the unpleasant question.

"Everybody always thinks that because of the way I look I know all about that kind of stuff."

"Don't you?" Chance asked.

Ray sighed as if the truth was a painful thing.

"Just between us, I won't deny that I purchase an occasional amount for personal consumption, and I may infrequently retail a little bit to friends. But I am by no reasonable stretch of the term a drug dealer."

"You never sell to your friends around here?"

"No, never!" Ray made a vague gesture of crossing his heart.

"How about using yourself? Ever do that around here?"

Ray paused and leaned against the soda machine. "You know how it is, dude, sometimes the body is weak, and I can spend ten hours a day here when we're short-handed. Occasionally. I'll go outside and light up. But I never use anything stronger when I'm on the job."

"But even that might be enough to get you fired."

He shrugged. "You know how these corporate types are. They aren't inclined to cut you any slack."

"So that was your dilemma, wasn't it?"

"How's that?"

"Hildie knew that you were using on the station grounds, and she was going to turn you in unless you helped her with the documentary."

Ray shook his head and groaned.

"It was worse than that, man. She had pictures of me smoking right outside the back door. Beautiful shots. She got her pet weasel, Sam, to take them with a telephoto. Shots so clear that you could see the joint in my hand. I suppose I could have claimed it was a plain old cigarette, but everyone knows that I don't smoke. That stuff is bad for your health."

"Sounds like Hildie had you between a rock and a hard place."

"The woman is ruthless. I don't know what happened to her at home growing up. She's got nothing but blind ambition left in her. And she doesn't care what she does to people to get what she wants."

"What exactly did she want you to do?"

"She wanted me to go out on the street at night and make a couple of buys. She and Sam would be running surveillance from a van and getting shots to use for the opening of her great documentary. I told her she could find stock footage, but Hildie wanted it to take place at some recognizable spot in Springfield."

"Was she going to conceal your identity?"

"Yeah, that's what she said. But who could trust her? The woman has no journalistic integrity, you know. If she liked a picture that had my whole face hanging out there in front of the camera, it would go on air, and she'd think nothing of it. She wouldn't even give me a heads up that it was going to happen. Or what if she started bragging to a couple of her friends about her big story and happened to throw my name around? The next time I go out to buy, I could end up with a couple of broken legs."

"So you turned her down?"

"Not exactly. I just suggested to her that she might get a more interesting story if she used Travis as her front guy."

"You knew he sold drugs?"

Ray nodded. "I'd heard it on the street. People told me because they knew I worked with him. He dealt with guys a couple of levels up from the ones I used because he was really buying to sell. Everybody knew who he was. He was sort of an idiot, you know, a guy with a well-known face buying drugs. How stupid do you get? They even had a nickname for him. They called him Stormy Weather, like "here comes Stormy Weather lookin' to score." A guy with a good job and a reputation dabbling in that stuff, what was he thinking? It was only a matter of time before he'd get picked up."

"He was doing more than dabbling, wasn't he?"

"Yeah, I guess he was pulling in some serious cash. But still, was it worth it?"

"Do you know who he made his purchases from?"

Ray shrugged. "Somebody way above my head. A guy you never see out on the street."

"Whom did Travis sell to?" I asked.

"Probably yuppies like himself that hang out in clubs around Springfield, maybe up in Northampton. They prefer to buy from one of their own. It makes them feel safer and less illegal."

Chance sat down on the edge of the table. "Did Hildie approach Travis after she talked to you?"

"I guess so."

"And he agreed to do it?"

"She never came back to me, so I guess he did."

"Why would he do that? Did Hildie have something on him, too?" I asked.

Ray shrugged. "Travis wanted to get into the news side of things, so maybe he thought a little undercover work would look good on his resume. Who knows with that dude? He was all screwed up."

On that, all three of us could agree.

****

I pulled up in front of the real estate office. It was at the far end of a mall where all the shops other than a woebegone pizzeria had already gone out of business. A small removable sign in the front window read Macdonald Realty. When I pushed open the door, a shrill bell rang.

The front room held a couple of plastic chairs and a table with a computer. Posters from around the world covered the walls. Since Bud Macdonald certainly wasn't selling properties in Europe and Asia, it led me to wonder whether this had formerly been a travel agency, and he just hadn't bothered to redecorate. There was the squeak of a chair in the back somewhere, and he came out to the front with a big smile on his face, ready to greet a potential customer. His smile disappeared immediately when he saw me.

"Not happy to see me, Mr. Macdonald?" I asked.

"Of course I am," he protested, coming forward and shaking my hand.

A round man, shorter than my five-eight, he looked up at me with a polite smile.

"I was just hoping it might be new business."

"Not selling many houses?"

"Things are deader than dead." He shook his head. "You understand how it is in this economy, people are afraid to buy. And with people walking away from their mortgages and builders still putting up new places, the market is saturated with inventory."

"The economy will turn around soon, I expect."

"That's what they say," Mr. Macdonald replied doubtfully.

"Once that happens the entire real estate market will improve." I was trying to cheer him up.

Even though economists often said that a rising economy raised all boats, I had doubts about the viability of Mr. Macdonald's craft. People looking to buy a house would take one look at his transient office quarters and feel they could do much better at some comfortable, nicely decorated realty agency. This was leaving aside the fact that Mr. Macdonald himself did not seem to have the resilient optimism necessary to his profession.

"Even the rental market is depressed," he continued, warming to the subject. "Rents have gotten so expensive and jobs so scarce that young single people are moving back home with their parents. I used to make good money buying old, run down houses and restoring them for sale or rent. But just try to get a bank loan to do that now. You'd think banks weren't in the business of giving loans anymore. Even with good collateral, when you go in and ask for a loan they look at you like you've got two heads."

I nodded sympathetically.

"Does that mean you won't be able to continue work on my garage?"

The man gave a moan that startled me. At first, I thought he was ill.

"That's another problem. I've actually got the money to complete that project, but the police won't let me continue building. They keep saying that the scene has to be maintained as is because Lambert's murder is an ongoing case. But what if they never solve it? I keep asking Lieutenant Green that, and all he tells me is not to worry, they're going to solve it eventually."

By putting the blame on me, I thought.

"But to tell you the truth, I'm not sure I'd go ahead with it even if I could. Now that the house is associated with a murder, who is going to want to live there?"

I thought that was an interesting question to be directing at me, the current tenant. Bud seemed to suddenly become aware of this because his usually pale face reddened.

"Not that there's anything wrong with the place. It's a fine house," he hurried on. "What difference does a murder make in the condition of the building? It's all in the mind. Sensible folks ignore that stuff."

"Well, fortunately, I have no intention of moving," I said.

I even surprised myself with that announcement, realizing that if I avoided prison I really did intend to stay in the house. A streak of stubbornness had kicked in, and I was determined not to let whoever had killed Travis drive me out of the house I liked.

Macdonald gave me a relieved smile. "I'm certainly glad to hear that. When I first saw you out here, I was sure you were going to try to break your lease." He paused for a moment. "Not that I think you could, but I'd hate to have to tell you that."

"No, I'm here because I wanted to learn more about Travis Lambert."

Bud gave me a surprised glance. "You worked with him, so you probably knew him better than I did."

"Well, we didn't exactly work together. We were on different shifts. And I heard that you and Travis were friends."

"Not friends, exactly. Travis used to work for me. A couple of years back when he first moved into the area and had just started at the station, he was looking for some extra money. I gave him some part-time work restoring houses I was rehabbing at the time. In fact, one of the last ones he worked on is the house you're living in. Travis spent quite a bit of time working on those renovations. He had real talent. I had hoped he'd keep working for me, but right after he finished your house, he said other activities had come up that took most of his free time."

A wild thought occurred to me. "Would he have had access to the keys to my house?"

"Sure, when he was working there I gave him a key. But I was very careful to see that it was returned to me once the work was done."

"But he could have made a copy?"

"I suppose," Macdonald admitted reluctantly. "Do you think Travis was coming into your house when you weren't home? Did you notice stuff being disturbed or missing?"

"No, nothing like that. But I'm just trying to figure out why he would have been at my house on the night he was murdered."

"I just figured the two of you were…friends."

"Well, we weren't. We were hardly colleagues," I said.

"Oh, then I can see why it might be a puzzle."

"What about the cellar? Would he have had a key?"

"We put a new lock on the outside cellar door in the back. I suppose he could have made a copy of that. But why would he?"

Why, indeed? Was it possible that he had been heading for the back door to the cellar on the night he was killed?

"Did the police come to see you about getting a key so they could search the cellar?"

Macdonald shook his head. "Do you think we should check it out?"

"I definitely do. Would it be all right if the private detective who's on the case and myself were there with you?"

"I guess so. I don't expect to find anything, but it might be just as well if I had some witnesses along in case something happens to turn up."

"I checked my watch. "I have to get back to the station now. What if we got together at the house at three o'clock."

Macdonald agreed, and I left, wondering if I was going to finally have an answer as to why Travis had died in my backyard.

Chapter Nineteen

"I need to tell you about what I found out from Bud McDonald," I said softly to Chance as he stood by the reception desk smiling at Mia.

"Give me a few minutes. Mia said that Slobo Krankovich is here, and I want to talk to him."

"*We'll* talk to him," I corrected.

"Of course," he said with a patient smile.

As we walked down the hall, we heard shouting coming from Clarissa Hayes' office. The door flew open just as we approached, and Clarissa came out into the hall, bumping into Malone. Ignoring him, she turned back to someone still in the office.

"I wish you would stop acting like such a fool and get a handle on your imagination. If this keeps going on, I really will leave you."

"Don't talk like that, Clarissa," a man's deep voice pleaded. "You know I act this way only because I love you."

We peered into the office and saw a short brawny man standing in the middle of the room with his arms outstretched.

"That's Slobo," I whispered to Chance.

"Would you happen to be Slobodan Krankovich?" Malone asked.

"That's who he is all right," Clarissa answered.

"Your husband?" asked Malone.

"For the moment. What do you want to see him about?"

"He knew Travis, and I'm trying to talk to everyone around here who did."

She glanced back in the office where the man now stood with his hands down at his sides, a sheepish expression on his face.

"Good luck having an intelligent conversation with him," Clarissa said, turning and stalking off down the hall.

We entered the office, and Malone closed the door behind us.

"I know who you are. You're that weather girl," Krankovich said to me. He turned to Malone. "But who are you?" he growled, peering up at him from under heavy eyebrows.

"Chance Malone." Malone stuck out his hand, but it was ignored. "I'm a private detective investigating the death of Travis Lambert."

"The little sneak was always hanging around my Clarissa. I warned him that if he didn't leave her alone, I'd spoil his pretty face for him. He just laughed, so I hit him in the stomach. That stopped his laughing."

Malone leaned against the door and gave a lazy smile.

"And maybe the other night you decided to follow him and get him alone to make good on your threat to rearrange is face. But things got a little out of hand, and before you knew it, he ended up dead."

"You are accusing me of murder."

The man's hands became fists the size of hams, and he suddenly charged forward. Malone seemed surprised by the outburst of violence, and only had the opportunity to shove his left hand out in front of him in the direction of Krankovich's face. As luck would have it, the heel of his hand came into hard contact with the point of Slobo's chin. Slobo stopped instantly, a dreamy expression came over his face, and before Malone could catch him, he crumpled to the floor.

"You've just knocked out the Killer of Croatia," I said.

"Apparently the Killer has a glass jaw."

Malone went over to the desk and poured a glass of water from a carafe. He came back and poured some of it carefully over the unconscious man's face. Slobo soon began to splutter, that turned to muttering. Malone stepped back, ready for a renewal of the conflict. But when Slobo's eyes cleared, and he sat up, he looked at Malone with respect.

"You knocked me out," he said in an amazed voice. "No one has ever done that before."

Probably because you're a bully who always gets in the first punch, I thought.

"It was an accident," said Malone. "Don't take it personally."

The man climbed to his feet and on rubbery legs made his way to the chair.

"You don't look tough. You look like just another one of those pretty boys." Slobo laughed. "But I guess you can't always judge a book by its cover."

"So they say," Malone replied. "Now how about telling me if you saw Travis Lambert on the night of his murder."

Slobo shook his head. "I swear I did not. I hit him that one time, but that was early on when he first came here. I meant it merely as a warning. Later I began to see that he was not interested in Clarissa."

From Slobo's point of view that must have put Travis in a pretty exclusive group, I thought.

Malone smiled patiently. "From the stories I've heard, you don't need much reason to get violent. Maybe he insulted you in some way."

The man leaned forward until he almost toppled out of the chair. "You seem like an honest man. Can I tell you something in confidence? This means you, too, young lady," he said to me. I nodded quickly.

"As long as you're not admitting to a crime, I'll keep your secret," said Malone.

He waved away the idea that this was about a crime.

"I know that behind my back people call me the Killer of Croatia. All of that stuff is just based on a few hints I've purposely let drop about my past, but they are all lies. I've never been to Croatia. In fact, I haven't been back to Europe since I left as a teenager. I made my money selling real estate in New Jersey."

"So why the war criminal act?" asked Malone.

"It's just a way to frighten men, so they will stay away from Clarissa. A realtor from New Jersey frightens no one, but a Croatian war criminal is a person to reckon with."

"Do you really think she's unfaithful to you?" I asked.

He smiled. "Look at me. I know what else they say, that I look like a bear more than a man. Do you think I do not look in mirrors? Do you think I can't see? I know what they say is true. The happiest moment of my life was when Clarissa agreed to marry me. That was followed by the unhappiest when I realized that I must hang onto her. And that is what I have been working at ever since."

"So what got things started today?" asked Malone.

"The copier repairman came into the office. Clarissa was showing him what was wrong with the machine. I saw he was standing much too near her. When he showed her what button to push on the machine, I think his hand may have touched hers."

"And that made you jealous?" Malone asked.

"He should not have stood so close. I simply went over and suggested that he give the woman some room to breathe. He took offense and an argument broke out. The man left before I had to throw him out, but Clarissa is angry because now the copier is still not repaired."

"Maybe she's also angry because she doesn't like it when you don't trust her," I said.

Slobo stared at the hairy backs of his hands.

"Perhaps that is also true," he admitted.

"Maybe you should give your wife more space," I suggested. "After all, nothing is going to happen in the middle of a busy office."

"I suppose not."

"Is there anyone else around here with whom Travis had problems?" Malone asked.

Slobo shrugged his massive shoulders.

"Aside from his difficulties with Holly, Mia, and you," he said, looking at me, "which Clarissa has told me about. I do not know of anyone who has had particular problems with him. People occasionally found him hard to work with because he was a very vain young man. That is why I started to worry about him less as he was here longer. He could not be interested in Clarissa because he was too much in love with himself."

"What about his activities outside of work?"

"I know nothing about any of this. I have recently heard from my wife that he was involved in drugs, but this came as news to me."

Malone stood up. "Well, thanks for all the help. Are you sure you're okay?"

Slobo nodded. "You said that I should give Clarissa more space when she is in the office."

"That's right," I said.

"But what about when she is outside the office, and I am not around?"

"Then you have to trust her."

He shook his head and stared at Malone. "You are a private detective. Perhaps I could hire you to watch Clarissa when she is not at work or home with me."

"No, I don't think so, Slobo," Malone said, opening the door. "That isn't trust, that's surveillance."

When we were back in the hall, I grabbed Malone by the arm.

"We have to talk," I said, directing him to a quiet corner. "I saw Bud McDonald."

"Okay. What did you find out?"

"Travis was involved in the renovation of my house. I think that could be why he was in my backyard the night he died."

Malone looked puzzled. "I think you have to fill in the blanks. I'm not following you."

"You remember that the one part of the house I don't have access to is the basement. Well, what if Travis had a key to the outside door to the basement, and that's where he was heading when he was killed?"

Malone thought for a moment then a smile came

over his face.

"That would be brilliant. He could store his drug cache in your house, so if it ever did happen to be found, it couldn't be traced back to him."

"He'd have easy access every night until eleven because I'm not home, and even after that, with all the noise the furnace makes, I'd never hear someone in the basement if he was reasonably quiet."

"We've got to check out that cellar."

"I'm way ahead of you," I said. "We're supposed to meet Bud over at my place at three o'clock. He's going to open the door so we can look around. Do you think we should have the police there?"

"They made a big mistake by not checking it out themselves. Let's have a look first to make sure there's something worth showing them."

Chance gave me a big smile, and my heart tightened. I really have it bad for this guy. Then came the cold rush of disappointment. Too bad we're not better suited. But then I remembered Gloria's warning that I shouldn't try to think too far ahead. Go out with him once and see what happened. I had a feeling about what would happen. I'd be attracted like crazy to him more than ever, and the religion issue would still be standing there between us.

I checked my watch. "I have to hurry to do my two o'clock update. See you later."

"I'll meet you at your house."

I hurried into the bullpen and over to my desk. I gathered the data for the day's forecast and sent it through to Maggie's computer. I was about rush across the hall to the studio when I happened to look out the window over my desk. Out near the tree line beyond the parking lot, I saw Ray talking to a very large man. It was too far away to be sure, but he looked a lot like the thug working for Mr. Adams. When I walked into the studio, Maggie was standing by the camera impatiently tapping her foot.

"Where is that boy? All I ask him to do it to be on time, and yet he wanders off right when we have something to do."

The back door of the studio flew open, and Ray ran in, out of breath.

"Sorry, there was something I had to take care of, and I got delayed."

Delayed consorting with criminals. I was tempted to confront him about it but decided to talk it over with Malone first.

When we were done, and Ray had disappeared into the break room, I leaned against Maggie's desk.

"Did you know that Travis was involved in the renovation of the house where I live?"

"No. I knew that he had done that kind of work for a while when he started at the station, but I wasn't aware of how long it continued."

I lowered my voice. "I think he was using my basement to store drugs."

Maggie's jaw went slack.

"You don't really think he was into that kind of thing in such a big way, do you?"

I put a hand on Maggie's shoulder. "I know you don't like to think badly of the people who work here. But I believe he was more involved in drug dealing than you ever suspected."

Tears formed in Maggie's eyes, and she brushed them away. Not for the first time, I realized that even though she was only a few years older than I, she was everyone's mother, worrying and caring for them.

"Well, I'll be very sorry if that turns out to be true. But at least it will help explain to the police why Travis was at your house on the night he died. That should make them less suspicious of you."

"I hope so. Malone and I are going over to my house in a little while to meet with my landlord and see what we can find in the basement."

"Well, for your sake I hope there's some evidence that Travis was using the space to store his drugs. We can't do anything to help him, but at least we can hope to help you."

"Thanks, Maggie. And remember orthoclase feldspar."

Maggie gave me a small smile. "Yes, good luck to you, too."

I walked back to the bullpen. Standing by their desks in the middle of the room were Hildie and Sam. They were going over some still photos and talking quietly together. Since Hildie was mostly out on the road, this was a good opportunity to question her. I walked over and stood nearby until Hildie looked up. Her sharp chin jutted forward.

"Can I help you?" she asked in her usual strident voice. Always anticipate an insult was her motto.

"I hope so. Can I speak to you alone for a minute?" I asked, giving Sam an apologetic smile. I thought for a moment she was going to refuse, but then she gave Sam a quick nod. He must have known what that meant for he immediately headed down the hall to the break room.

"What do you want?" she asked.

"I've heard that you tried to get Ray to help you with a drug exposé you were planning to produce. And when he refused to help you, you turned to Travis."

She gave me a wintry smile. "You hear a lot of things around here. As they say in politics, I can neither confirm nor deny."

I tamped down my anger and made my voice as cool as hers.

"That's your privilege. But if you don't talk to me, I'll go to Clarissa and ask if she knew anything about this little plan of yours. Maybe I'll even bring the matter to Lieutenant Green. I'm sure he'd be interested to know that you were soliciting Travis to buy drugs for you. That should make you part of a murder investigation.

"It wasn't like that, and you know it. I didn't want the drugs for myself," Hildie shot back.

I could sense fear beneath the anger.

"I won't know how it was unless you talk to me. If I go away satisfied, no one has to find out about this."

Hildie paused for a moment, then her face took on a look of resignation. "There's nothing to tell you. I thought Ray would jump at the chance to be in front of the camera for a change and do some journalism. And I wasn't asking him to do something that he didn't already do most Friday nights. I promised I'd blur his face, so no one would recognize him, but he got nervous about the idea of being on camera. He was afraid of some of these drug dealers and didn't want anything to do with exposing them. I couldn't convince him that there was almost no risk."

"So you went to Travis?"

"I didn't even know he was into drugs until Ray

told me. So I talked to him and made the same offer I'd made to Ray."

"What happened?"

"I could see that he really liked the idea of being on camera. He had some interest in switching over to the journalistic side. But I couldn't convince him to work with me either. He said that the guys he dealt with were a couple of levels up from anyone we'd find on the street, and if he got filmed making a buy, they'd find out it was him, and he'd be in a lot of trouble. I tried to change his mind, but he was really scared. In fact, by the time I got done talking to him, I wasn't sure I wanted to get into something that heavy myself."

"So Travis turned you down. Did you tell anybody that you'd asked him to make a buy on camera?" I asked, wondering if word could have gotten back to Travis' supplier that he was even considering an on-air buy.

"Sam knew. That's all."

"Did Sam tell anyone?"

"He knows better."

"Could you check?"

She sighed, and went down the hall to the break room. In a minute she was back. "Sam didn't tell anyone either."

I tapped my foot and tried to think of something else to ask.

"If that's all, I've got things to do," Hildie said, picking some papers off her desk.

"What happened with your drug exposé?"

"Nothing. We canned it. The whole drug scene has been overdone anyway, and I couldn't come up with a new angle. I decided instead to go with an investigation of the auto repair business." Suddenly her eyes lit up, and she reached forward as if to grab me by the lapels. "How would you like to be part of it? I'm looking for young single women willing to take a car that we've already had checked out and certified to be in great condition into a garage and say you hear a strange sound. Then we're going to see if the mechanic makes up something to fix. Want to give it a try?"

"Sounds a little deceptive to me."

"Some of the best journalism is. We're just running a little sting. Nobody honest is going to get hurt."

I wasn't so sure of that. Gotcha journalism didn't appeal to me.

"I think I'll give it a pass."

Hildie gave me a contemptuous what-can-you-expect look and went off to find Sam.

As I walked back to my desk, I wondered whether I would ever become like Hildie. Not in the sense of being deceptive, but allowing my ambition to get in the way of being a good person. Was I a good person now? In some odd way, the death of Travis Lambert was forcing me to reexamine my life. I suspected that if it hadn't been Travis' death, it would have been something else. The time was ripe for me to make decisions about my future.

Chapter Twenty

At two-thirty I drove down the hillside toward Ridley and the meeting at my house with Bud McDonald. As I drove, my thoughts drifted to Travis. Hard to believe he was as involved in drug dealing as the evidence seemed to indicate. I had always associated drug dealing with large, violent men whose bodies were covered with tattoos, the stereotypical image of the rogue biker.

Travis had been clean cut, well educated, and would have fit perfectly in any middle class context. That was what made him a successful dealer. He was most likely dealing to other young executive types who would never go near a tough-looking criminal but were happy to buy from one of their own. Buying from Travis, they were able to convince themselves that what they were doing wasn't linked to killings around the world, but was an innocent recreational activity. And Travis, for his part, had convinced himself that what he was doing was an acceptable way of making money because he was providing a service to his friends and nobody, at least nobody he saw, got hurt.

I went around the circle at the green thinking that no one would suspect such a peaceful place could harbor so much crime. I figured, people were much the same everywhere, prone to do wrong when tempted, but also capable of good.

I swung south off the circle and headed toward home. As I pulled onto my street, I saw Malone's car in front of my house. He was sitting in it, apparently waiting for me. An SUV that I assumed belonged to Bud McDonald was in the driveway. I pulled in beside Bud and hopped out of the car. Malone got out of his car and came over to meet me.

"I didn't want to go into the house until you got here because I don't know Bud. Under the circumstances, he might be jumpy about a stranger walking in on him."

"Bud's so down right now because of the economy that he'd probably just give a loud groan."

We walked up to the front door and found it locked. I opened the door, and we went inside. In the kitchen, I tried the door to the basement, but it was still firmly locked.

"I guess he used the outside door," I said. "Do you hear anything in the basement?"

Malone shook his head. "But there could be a herd of wild elephants down there. Who can hear anything over that furnace fan?"

"Let's go outside and check the door," I suggested.

Going out through the side door, we walked around to the back of the house. The door to the cellar was closed, but when Malone turned the handle, the door opened, revealing a set of steep stone steps.

"I'll go first," he said, starting down the stairs.

When we got to the bottom, there was another door. When Malone pushed it open, a strong smell of mustiness and mold greeted us. Malone felt around and found a switch. A couple of dim naked bulbs came on, revealing a large empty room.

"Not much of interest here," I said.

"No Bud either," Malone added.

He pointed to a crude wooden wall that separated part of the basement from the rest. The rattling of the furnace could be heard from the next room. Malone walked over and opened a door that had been cut into the wall. There was nothing but darkness. Malone took out a flashlight and shined it around inside the room. He found a switch and another light came on. I followed Malone and found Bud McDonald lying face down next to the furnace. Malone knelt beside him. Bud moaned slightly when Malone rolled him over.

"Find something to put under his head," Malone shouted over the noise of the furnace. He took out his cell phone and pointed into the next room. "I'm going to call for an ambulance and the police."

I folded up an old blanket I found in a corner and put it under Bud's head. He said a few indistinct words. Suddenly the furnace went silent.

Chance came back in the room. "I turned the heat off, so we can hear ourselves think."

"What do you think is wrong with him?" I asked.

He bent over Bud. "Hard to tell. I don't see any blood. Could be a heart attack or a stroke, but he seems to be breathing fine, and his heartbeat is strong."

Malone began to look around the room. It was about ten feet by fifteen, and much of the center of it was filled with the old furnace. But over in one corner was a cabinet. The hasp and padlock had been pried off. Inside were plastic bags of something that looked like white powder. Malone went over and took a look.

"What's that?" I asked.

"I think we've found Travis' stash of drugs."

"So he did hide drugs in my basement," I said, getting angry at the dead man all over again. "That means he took advantage of renovating my house to have a cellar key made, and he's been sneaking down here ever since I've lived in the place. He must have enjoyed threatening me at work, while at the same time he was turning my house into a drug dump." I shivered. "That's so creepy."

"But smart. No one was ever going to find drugs in his possession unless they actually caught him transporting them on his person, and he probably only carried drugs when he was making a sale."

"So what was he doing here on the night he was killed?"

"I think that, along with his drugs, he had also hidden the statues here. Why wouldn't he? It was the safest place he knew. Mr. Adams could toss his apartment as often as he wanted, and he wouldn't find anything. Remember he was supposed to meet Adams that night to sell the statues back to him. I think he came here to get them with every intention of keeping that appointment.

"But instead he got killed," I said. "So who killed him? If he was going to make the deal with Adams, it couldn't be him."

"Not likely. Unless they followed him to make sure he had the stuff, then killed him to avoid paying. But then they'd have the statues, which we know they don't or else they'd be long gone."

"So this doesn't really help us find the killer?"

"Nope."

We heard the siren from a vehicle pulling up in front of the house. A few minutes later a voice called "hello" down the stairwell. Malone directed them down to Bud. The EMTs, a man and a woman, asked us what we knew about his injuries, then put him on a stretcher.

"Is anyone going to the hospital with him?" the woman asked.

We looked at each other.

"You go," said Malone. "You know him better. I'll stay here and talk to the police. Follow the ambulance in your own car. That way you can come back whenever you want."

I gave him a wave and walked behind the stretcher up the stairs.

Ten minutes later, I followed the ambulance into the emergency room parking at Ridley Community Hospital. I trailed along behind the EMTs as they pushed the stretcher in through the automatic door, but I was required to wait at the admissions desk while they took Bud into the treatment room. The woman at admissions asked me for Bud's name. Fortunately, Bud had been to the hospital before, so his name was enough to bring up all his personal information on the computer screen. A good thing, since I knew very little about the man. I told the woman that we had found him unconscious but had no idea what had happened. After several more minutes, she printed out a series of forms.

"Can I see him now?" I asked.

"And what is your relationship to the patient?"

I searched around for the most truthful answer that would work. He's my landlord, didn't sound quite close enough.

"We're business associates," I replied, giving her one of my best smiles.

"Let me check."

I stood there for a good five minutes before the woman returned.

She motioned me through the door then said, "C'mon, I'll show you where he is."

The woman led me down a hall and pointed to a room at the end. Bud was lying on a metal gurney, and a young woman who was a nurse or an aide of some sort was attaching a monitor to his arm. He'd been put in a hospital gown, which made him look older and more vulnerable. However, he was awake and glancing around. I waited until the woman left before approaching him.

"How are you feeling, Bud?" I asked, bending over in front of his face.

He looked at me with curiosity.

"What are you doing here?"

"Don't you remember, we were going to meet this afternoon in the basement at my house."

"I remember," Bud said after a long pause. "But how did I get here?"

"You got to the house ahead of me. When I went down in the basement, you were on the floor unconscious. I guess you decided not to wait for me to begin looking around."

I caught a shrewd and very aware look in Bud's eyes.

"I had some time, so I decided to start early," he said.

"Right," I said and made an intuitive leap. "Wasn't it more the case that you wanted to get rid of any incriminating evidence before I got there?"

Bud tried to look the picture of injured innocence, but couldn't quite pull it off in his diminished state.

He sighed. "Okay, I admit it. After you talked to me, I began to think that maybe you were right, and Travis was hiding drugs in the basement. I knew if the police found out about them, it would be all over the news. The newspaper might even give the address of the house, and then I'd never be able to lease it again. It would be like trying to rent a crack house, not to mention that the neighbors would be furious with me. And none of it is my fault. I never thought Travis was the kind of guy to get into something like that."

I put a soothing hand on Bud's arm.

"People forget, Bud. People forget quickly."

Bud shook his head. "Maybe, maybe not. The neighbors would remember. Who knows what they'd say to a potential renter who asked around?"

"So when you pried the lock off the cabinet and found the drugs, what were you going to do with them? Throw them away before I got there?"

"What drugs?" Bud began feverishly rubbing his face with his hands. "Oh, no! You mean there really were drugs there?"

"You didn't find them?"

"I didn't get a chance to find anything. I went down the stairs. I opened the door to the room where the furnace is. I was just thinking to myself that you were right, and I should get someone to fix the fan on that furnace when I felt a sharp pain in my right shoulder. It went all the way through my body and the next thing I knew I was on the floor. Then I must have blacked out for a while. What happened to me? Did I have a heart attack? A stroke?"

Before I could say any more, a man entered the room. I figured he was a doctor or a physicians' assistant because a nurse followed him attentively. He introduced himself as Tom Clark, an emergency room doctor. He asked me to leave the room for a few moments while he examined Bud. I walked out into the hall and thought about Bud trying to hide the evidence of Travis' drug dealing. I was glad he didn't have the opportunity because this proved that Travis had a reason to be at my house that had nothing at all to do with me. Bud was lucky, in a way, that his plan to remove the drugs hadn't worked, or he'd be in trouble. This way he was an innocent victim. Bud wasn't a bad guy; he was just an extremely nervous and worried one.

A few minutes later the nurse called me back into the examining room.

"Do you know what's wrong with him?" I asked.

The doctor looked at me and smiled. "I almost missed it. I certainly wouldn't have caught it except that I worked for a while at the police academy. You know all officers have to be tasered."

"Is that what happened to Bud?"

The doctor pulled back the hospital gown and pointed to two angry red spots on the top of Bud's right shoulder.

"That's always a giveaway. The entry points of the electricity always leave a little burn mark."

"Would that have been enough to put him out?"

"A man of his size and age, sure. And even when he came around he'd be confused and disoriented for a while."

"Am I going to be all right?" Bud asked weakly.

"You're going to be fine," the doctor reassured him. "The worst you had to worry about was falling and hitting your head. There's no sign of that. Aside from a few scrapes and bruises on your knees and elbows, you look good. Your blood pressure and heart seem fine. Since it appears that a crime has been committed, the police will be here in a little while to talk to you."

After a few more words of reassurance, he left the room.

"You have no idea who attacked you?" I asked.

"Didn't even know anyone else was there. It's terrible when a man gets that kind of thing done to him in his own basement."

"That's what happens when you don't keep a close eye on your properties."

"What do you mean?"

"Well, if you are going to seal off the basement from your tenant, at least you should come around once in a while to check on the mechanicals. Then you might have spotted the cabinet where Travis hid his drugs. But Travis felt confident that you'd never check."

Bud nodded. "I suppose you're right. I have been neglecting the furnace. I promise I'll have someone look at it by the end of the week."

"Is there anyone I can call to come to take you home? I have to go to work in a little while."

Bud began to reach in his back pocket then realized he was in his underwear.

"Where are my pants? I need my wallet?"

I opened a metal closet in the corner and got Bud his wallet. He took out a folded slip of paper.

"Here, call this number. He's my nephew, but he's a good kid. He'll pick me up."

"The police are going to want to talk to you before you leave."

"What should I tell them?"

"The truth. Don't elaborate on it. Tell them that Malone and I found drugs there, but you never saw them. If they ask whether I had access to the basement, tell them I didn't. Make sure you explain how it was possible for Travis to have a key. Do you understand?"

"Okay."

"Now I'll give your nephew a call. Don't worry; he'll have plenty of time to get here. Nothing ever happens fast in the emergency room unless you're about to die. You'll probably be here for a couple more hours.

Since they didn't allow cell phone use in the emergency room, I went out into the parking lot to make my call. The man who answered had a young voice but said he'd be right over to help his Uncle Bud.

I stood in the parking lot for a moment watching the traffic pass by and wondered whom I would get to take me home under similar circumstances. I decided I'd probably have to take a taxi.

****

I sat in my living room and stared at Lieutenant Green. A scowling Green had been waiting for me when I returned home from the hospital. He chased Malone outside when I arrived and now sat across from me on the edge of my sofa, looking about as comfortable as if he expected it to burst into flames at any moment. He had demanded that I tell him the entire story from the top. I had. Now that I was done, he stared hard at me.

"So what do you know about these drugs in the basement?"

"Nothing that I haven't already told you," I replied.

"Then why did you suddenly ask McDonald to

give you access to the cellar?"

"When I went to talk to him about his relationship with Travis, he told me that Travis had been involved in the renovation of the house. That got me wondering if Travis had a key. When I found out he did, I thought it might be worthwhile to check the one area of the house I don't have access to—the basement."

"Where it turns out Travis was storing drugs."

"And that must explain why he was killed in my back yard. He was going down in the cellar to either pick up or return some drugs when he was attacked."

"If someone killed him to get access to his stash, why didn't they take it?"

"I don't know the answer to that any more than I know the answer to why the person who attacked Bud today didn't remove the drugs."

Green leaned forward even further until he was about to fall off the sofa.

"What it tells me is that this murder had nothing to do with drugs. It was a crime of passion."

"Well if it was, it had nothing to do with any passion between Travis and myself. We were not in any kind of relationship."

"So you say."

"Yes, I do," I snapped.

Lieutenant Green leapt to his feet.

"If this was a crime of passion, you're doing yourself no favor by denying it. From what I've learned about this Lambert guy, he wasn't much into being faithful. I imagine you had a secret relationship with him, just like this Debbie. I can understand how a sensitive woman like yourself might be very hurt if you discovered Lambert had dropped you for someone else.

Maybe you even found out he was using your house for a drug drop. You confronted him when he came that night to use the cellar. You accused him of being an unfaithful, manipulative crook. He laughed at you, and you picked up a rock and hit him. Any jury would be sympathetic to that. But you've got to come clean with me now, or I swear I'll throw the book at you."

For one brief, crazy, frightened moment I thought that confessing to something I hadn't done might be the best course of action. Then I came to my senses.

"I have come clean with you, Lieutenant, and I have nothing more to say."

Shaking his head sadly, as if sorry about what the consequences of my action were going to be, Green left the house. I sat on the sofa feeling slightly sick. I had thought that discovering the drugs would link Travis' death to the drug trade and take the heat off me. Instead, he was twisting it to be further proof that I had killed him. What could I do? I toyed with the idea of telling Green about the statues but figured that would just get me in more trouble for concealing evidence and probably not help my situation. He would just add theft to the murder charges he was already typing up.

There was a soft knocking at my front door. I went to open it, dreading the sight of Green's face. Instead, Malone stood there smiling. I stood back and let him in.

"So how did it go with Green?" he asked, replacing the lieutenant on the sofa but looking more relaxed.

I described the interrogation. When I was done, Malone nodded.

"I can see his point, and I'm inclined to agree with him that Travis' death had nothing to do with drugs."

"So you think it was a crime of passion, too?" I

said, exasperated.

"Possibly," he said, smiling at my angry face. "However, unlike Green, I know that there was no relationship, secret or otherwise, between you and Travis."

"Thank you for that at least. Do you think there was some woman who wanted him dead?"

"We've already eliminated Mia because she had an alibi."

"What about Debbie? Maybe she killed him because he dropped her for someone else?"

Chance shook his head. "I think we both agree that she still has this idealized picture of Travis as faithful and true. In another month she might have wanted to kill him, but not just yet."

"She could be lying," I said.

"If so, she's very good at it."

I shrugged. "So we have a mystery woman. And how does she tie in with the statues of our friend Indra and his buddies."

"I'm not sure."

"There's also the problem of the attack on Bud."

"Attack? What are you talking about?" Chance asked.

"Bud was tasered," I said. "How would somebody get one of them?"

"They're illegal in this state, but people buy them over the internet. Most people want them for self-defense, but it can be an effective weapon. Still, the whole thing strikes me as odd."

"What 'whole thing'?"

"The fact that Bud was tasered. I would normally suspect Mr. Adams and his friend were behind this.

They could have hired a second thug to follow you in addition to me, and then, when he saw you go to Bud's, he might have followed Bud to the house. Or maybe Adams has your house staked out.

I shivered at the thought.

"So if they spotted Bud going down in the cellar, I could see them wanting to find what might be hidden there. But now I don't think Adams had anything to do with it."

"Why not?"

"First of all, I think Mr. Adams would probably have taken the drugs. Even though that's not what he imports and exports, he'd probably know how to get some money for them. But maybe the amount just wouldn't be worth it to him. So I'm not sure about that one. My second reason is a better one."

"Which is?"

"I don't think one of Adams' thugs would use a stun gun They would have hit McDonald on the back of the head or banged his head against a wall. Somebody who uses a stun gun is trying to avoid inflicting injury. I don't think that's a major concern for Adams' employees.

"So a caring thug put Bud down?"

"Or at least one who didn't want to risk a murder charge."

"But can't a stun gun kill someone?"

"Sure, if they already have a weak heart or the person falls the wrong way. There's always a risk, but not as much as knocking someone out with a hard object."

I paused to put together in my mind what Malone was saying.

"So in addition to us, there are two other people looking for the gods of India—Mr. Adams and a mystery person."

"It seems that way to me."

"And there's also a mystery person who killed Travis. Are they the same person or two different people?"

"That's what we have to find out."

"I saw Ray talking to someone outside the station who looked like Mr. Adams' thug. Do you think he could be involved?"

Malone's eyes widened. "Hmm. I guess I need to have another chat with that boy."

I checked my watch. "I've got to get out of here, or I'll be late for my broadcast."

Malone got to his feet.

"Are you going to be okay staying alone here tonight?"

"You mean after yet another criminal attack on my property?" I smiled. "You know for the first time in a while, I feel safe here. I think knowing what's in the cellar has given me a greater sense of security. In a funny way, it's always bothered me that part of the house was sealed off."

"Okay," Malone said, opening the door. "I'll be in touch."

"What are you going to do next?

"I'll have to give it some thought."

"Let me know when you need my help."

He smiled, probably at my assumption the he would be needing it.

"I'll do that," he replied.

Chapter Twenty-One

I got up the next morning having had the best sleep I'd enjoyed in days. What I'd told Chance about feeling safer in the house had certainly turned out to be true. My good humor didn't last long as my mind drifted to Lieutenant Green. I had half expected him to come to the television station last night to arrest me, and I took his failure to appear to mean that he might be as stymied by the case as Chance and I were. As long as he didn't rush to judgment and arrest me, I was willing to give him all the time in the world.

As I went into the kitchen to put on the coffee and make some breakfast, I thought about Chance. When he'd left last night, he'd been uncertain as to when we'd meet again, and I was surprised to discover that seeing him was something I looked forward to. His charm and humor were a nice interlude in my somewhat humdrum life. He probably had other cases to solve, and I wouldn't hear from him until a new lead developed. I toyed briefly with the idea of calling and asking him out to an early lunch but nixed the idea because that would seem too much like a date. My friend Gloria would say that a date was just what I needed, but I still wasn't sure how close a relationship I wanted to have with him. Anyway, if I called him before my case was solved, he'd probably feel an obligation to go out with me as a professional courtesy. I wanted him to go out with me for myself alone, not from a sense of obligation.

The doorbell rang, and my stomach clenched. This could be the police here to put the cuffs on me. For a moment I considered not answering the door, but that seemed like postponing the inevitable. Walking slowly, telling myself to keep it together, I went down the front hall and opened the door.

A middle-aged woman stood there. She stared at me, and then gave me a tentative smile. The woman looked familiar, but not like someone I had ever met in real life. More like a celebrity that I'd seen on television or in the movies. One step removed from reality.

"Are you Stormy McCloud?" the woman asked.

"Yes."

"I'm your mother."

Both of us seemed uncertain what to do next. Finally, my mother put out her hand, and I politely shook it. She was wearing a conservative blue suit. I was surprised to see she wasn't wearing a caftan, love beads, and sandals.

"Please come in," I said, taking a step backwards out of the doorway, feeling momentarily dizzy.

As the woman walked past me, I recognized the scent and flashed back to a summer long ago when the two of us had rolled around together on the lawn behind the house. A time I hadn't thought about in many years.

"Would you like some coffee?" I asked when my mother was seated in the living room.

"Don't you think we'd better talk first? I'm sure you have a lot of questions you'd like to ask me. Why don't you just ask away, and I'll answer them as best I can."

I sat on the sofa feeling very much on the spot. Questions buzzed like angry bees in my mind, but it was difficult to seize one and bring it into focus. Finally, one question came to stand out from the rest.

"How could you run off and leave us like that?"

My mother nodded as if that were the question she had anticipated.

"That's a little hard even for me to understand looking back from the distance of twenty years. Let me ask you, have you ever been in love?"

"I've thought so once or twice, but I'm not really sure."

"Well, maybe I wasn't quite as sure at the time as I thought I was either. But when I left you and your father, I was absolutely certain that I'd found the love of my life. He was my soul mate. If I couldn't be with him, there was no point in going on."

"He must not have felt the same way, if he left you," I said harshly.

The woman smiled. "No. Oh, I think he thought that he loved me, but he wasn't ready to settle down and take the responsibility for a family. We were only in our twenties after all, and neither one of us was very mature."

"But you'd married my father just a few years before. Weren't you in love with him?"

"Of course. When I first met him, I was right out of college, and he was starting on his academic career. Your father is a brilliant mathematician, and from the first time I met him, I felt that he lived in completely different, more exalted, universe than the rest of us. When he would sit and suddenly go off somewhere in his mind, brooding over a mathematical concept, I thought it was so romantic that this special man wanted someone like me. Even though I never completely believed it, I felt that made me special, too. I was the one who could make him laugh and provide a home so he didn't have to worry about mundane things."

"What went wrong?" I asked.

"He loved mathematics more than he did me. He would come home after a day at school, eat a quick meal, and then go into his study for hours, most times staying up late into the night. He hardly talked to me, and I couldn't blame him. How much would I have been able to understand if he had shared his thoughts with me?"

"Couldn't you have talked about other things?"

"You know your father. He has very little tolerance for small talk."

"But didn't you try to get him to pay more attention to you?"

"Of course, I was always suggesting things to do in the evening: going to the movies, having dinner with people, just watching television together. I urged him to take a vacation in the summer so we could travel to new places. But all he wanted to do was work. When I pressed him on it, he got angry and said that the great mathematicians did their best work when they were young, and time was slipping away for him. He was a driven man."

"Didn't he change after you had me?" I asked.

"Initially, I think he was thrilled. It was a combination of curiosity at what you would turn out to be and the desire to teach you about the world, as he understood it. But the normal chores of tending to an infant held no charms for him. They were just a distraction from his work. He said you could be mine until the age of five, then he would start to mold you."

"And that's what happened, isn't it?"

"Yes, although I never planned for it to take place that way. If I hadn't met a handsome, charming assistant professor of English at the college athletic club looking for a tennis partner, your father and I probably would have reached some emotional accommodation and bumped along well enough together. But meeting someone who thought that I was worth his undivided attention opened my eyes. From then on my marriage felt like a straitjacket from which I had to escape. So when my English professor got a job teaching on the west coast, I jumped at the opportunity to start a new life."

"Your new life didn't last long."

"Only about six months. Like I said, we were both rather immature."

"Why didn't you come back to us when your relationship ended?"

"Your father had already initiated divorce proceedings. He didn't want me to come back. I was never sure whether his feelings had been too hurt or his pride too injured, but he wasn't about to forgive me."

"But you could have come back to see me," I said, trying to keep the hurt out of my voice.

"Your father got custody of you. Certainly, I had visitation rights on a couple of weekends a month, but that was difficult to negotiate from California."

"You could have moved back here and stayed part of my life."

Slowly my mother nodded her head. "I did come out to see you several of times during the first few years we were apart. I still can't fully explain it, but all I can say is that your father made it clear to me that I was a bad influence on you. He could be very convincing, and I was so filled with guilt by then that I was ready to believe him. I saw that he was devoted to you, and wasn't shutting you out of his life the way he did me. By then you were his project, and he told me that I would just be an awkward meddler."

"You should never have let that happen. A girl needs to have her mother."

"I know that, and if it were to happen today, I would be strong enough to stand up to him. But back then, I was still in awe of your father and believed he understood everything better than I did."

I sat silently, thinking over all she had said.

"Can I ask you a question?"

I nodded.

"When you got older why didn't you come out to see me? At least you could have called or written. I would have been happy to hear from you."

"I think my father had convinced me that beyond a Christmas and birthday present, you really didn't want to have anything to do with my life. Whenever anyone asked why I didn't contact you, he told me to say that I was waiting for you to make the first move."

My mother smiled and shook her head.

"The two of us have been very stupid in allowing ourselves to be manipulated by your father."

"If he's so horrible, why have you come back?"

"Because he's convinced me that he's changed. I know, of course, that he could just be manipulating me once more, but I'm willing to take that risk in order for us to be a family again. Plus, you have to understand, he's the only man I've ever really loved."

I paused for a moment, not sure what to say to that.

"What evidence do you have that he's changed?"

My mother laughed. "A logical question, just like your father would ask."

"Do you have an answer?"

"Your father is much older now. I think he's accomplished everything he can do creatively in mathematics. Now he's simply elaborating on ideas he had in his twenties and thirties. And he's come to realize that he doesn't want to be alone as he gets older. I think he's finally begun to understand that the emotional side of life is as necessary as the intellectual. He wants me back, and I think he's afraid that he's gradually losing you. He understands that he hasn't always made things easy for you by insisting that you follow in his footsteps."

"Is he willing to accept my decision to become a meteorologist?"

"He may never be happy with it, but I think he can accept that it was yours to make."

I wondered if that was actually true. It would be a hard concession for my father.

"So how is this going to work? Are the two of you just going to start living together again or are you going to get remarried? What will this be like from a practical point of view?"

"A very good question. We've been communicating by e-mail and phone for the past few months, tentatively working out what things would be like between us. What we've decided so far is that I'll move back to this area and find my own place. We'll start dating and see what happens from there. If we decide to live together, we'd both like the commitment of marriage to back it up. But both your father and I would want to have your support in doing this."

"You want my blessing?" I asked, almost smiling.

"We'd at least like you to give it as much of a chance as we are. We'd like to start doing things together as a family for the first time."

"I'm willing to do that if I can."

"What do you mean?"

"Hasn't my father told you that I may end up in prison?"

"Your father mentioned something about a colleague of yours being murdered, but he didn't say it concerned you."

"I guess he didn't want to worry you," I said, and for the first time since this whole thing had started, I began to choke up. A second later, two gentle arms enfolded me, and I turned to put my face deeply into my mother's shoulder. Then I cried for the first time since I was a little girl.

Chapter Twenty-Two

After my mother left, as I sat on the sofa trying to absorb all that had just happened, the phone rang. It was David Palmer.

"I just called to find out if we're still on for Sunday."

It took me a moment to register what he was talking about. With all that had been happening, I had forgotten about going to the reception at the college art gallery with David. But it still seemed like a good idea. I needed a diversion from my problems, and although I had thought of David more as a friend than a romantic interest, I reminded myself that nothing prevented friendship from developing into something more. Compared to Chance, he seemed less complicated.

"If you're still interested, I certainly am."

"Good. I just wanted to make sure. Have there been any new developments in the Travis Lambert murder investigation?"

I remembered Malone's warning not to share information with anyone, but at the same time, I didn't want to lie to David.

"We're really no closer to finding out who killed him," I replied, figuring that was a pretty accurate description of the current state of affairs.

"Have you decided what you're going to do with the statue?"

"Not yet. We'll have to see how things go. Have you heard any more from the FBI?"

"Not a word. But, like I told you before, I don't expect them to launch an investigation."

"Good."

"I'm just kind of curious as to where the rest of the statues went. You'd think if Travis had them, he'd have kept the entire set together."

"So far they haven't turned up, and we have no idea where they might be. Maybe the person who killed Travis took them."

"Then if you find the killer, you find the artwork?"

"Could be. But we don't know for sure."

"Well, I certainly hope it works out that way. Then I can call my friend at the FBI and give him a heads up as to where they are. That should impress them at the bureau."

"All I care about is finding the killer, so I'm off the hook."

"Of course, I understand. This must be a terrible worry for you. But on Sunday maybe I can take your mind off unpleasant things, at least for a while. I'll pick you up around ten-thirty. We'll go to brunch at the Water Wheel Inn, and then on to Doug Fowler's reception."

"Sounds great."

When we had said our goodbyes, I sat back in my chair and smiled. A normal date with an educated and attractive guy would make a nice change of pace from what had been going on this week. I could hardly believe that it had only been this last Tuesday when Travis' body had been found. Since then I'd been living in a prolonged nightmare. No, I would definitely have a good time on Sunday. I was determined that I would.

The phone rang again, and this time, it was Malone.

"Any new leads?" I asked.

"I'm going to question Ray again. I'll try to find out what's going on with him and Adams. I did an internet search on Deming, New Mexico. But aside from learning that it's in the southern part of New Mexico and known for its natural beauty, if you like desert, it didn't seem to offer much in the way of a lead. I even called Debbie to find out when her birthday is, but it's December, so the birthday card and the trip weren't meant for her. But given Travis' habit of having as many girlfriends as possible at the same time, it's hard to pin down the intended recipient of the card. Otherwise, I'm out of ideas for the moment."

"Have you tried consulting the Bible?" I asked, half-kidding.

There was a long silence. "Actually, I have. I just opened it up and pointed to a passage at random."

"What did it say?"

"My finger landed on Proverbs, chapter fifteen, verse twenty. 'A wise son maketh a glad father: but a foolish man despiseth his mother.'"

"Seems like a true observation," I said, not wanting to offend him.

"But not particularly helpful to the case. Nothing works all the time."

A wave of despair washed over me. "You know even if the police never arrest me and if this case is never solved it will always hang over me like a cloud. We have to find the real killer for me to be exonerated."

"We will," Malone said firmly. "We're just

temporarily at a dead end right now, but that usually happens right before things break wide open."

"I hope so."

"Get a good night's sleep. Are you coming to the station tomorrow even though it's a Saturday?"

"No, I have tomorrow and Sunday off. That's when I'm going out with David."

"That's right. I'd forgotten."

I had a feeling by the tone of his voice that Malone hadn't forgotten at all.

"What time do you go to work today?"

"The usual, early afternoon."

"Would you like to meet my nephew, Joshua? School is out today for some reason, and my sister is at work. I promised to drop by to visit him. It's right in your neighborhood, and we wouldn't have to stay long."

"Okay."

Malone arrived in fifteen minutes. It only took us five minutes before we were parked in the driveway of a small ranch house. We walked up on the front porch. When Chance rang the bell, we saw a boy peer cautiously from around the drape of the living room window to see who was at the door. Chance stood well back on the porch so he would be easy to recognize from inside. When Joshua spotted him his face broke into a smile, and he was at the front door in a second, scrambling to get it unlocked. Finally, the door opened, and Joshua ran out to give his uncle a hug.

"This is Ms. McCloud. She's a friend of mine."

I put out my hand.

"Hi, Joshua."

"Hi," he said, taking my hand and looking up at me

with something akin to awe. I wished the older boys treated me with that kind of respect.

"Want to play some catch?" Chance asked.

"Let me get my glove and ball," the boy said excitedly.

Chance had his own glove that he carried around in the car just in case he got the opportunity to play with Joshua, and soon they were in the backyard throwing the ball around. After warming up, Chance squatted down pretending to be a catcher. Joshua made believe that he was a pitcher and threw the ball as hard as he could, trying to put it right in the glove. Chance complimented him on the ones that were good and offered some advice when the ball was high, low, or outside. Even though Joshua was a bit small for his age, he had a good arm, and Chance had said on the way over that he wouldn't be surprised if his nephew got to pitch in Little League in a couple of years.

Finally, when they both were tired, we went into the kitchen and sat at the table drinking glasses of ice water. After talking about baseball for a few minutes, the boy became quiet.

"What are you thinking about, Champ?" Chance asked.

"I was wondering whether you ever think about getting married."

At first, I thought Chance was going to laugh it off. But the expression on Joshua's face must have told him that the boy seriously wanted to know.

"Of course, I think about it. I guess some day I will. Why?"

"Well, if you get married, you'll probably have children, right?"

"I suppose."

Joshua thought for a long moment. "If you had children, would you still come to play with me?"

"Sure, I would. I'll never stop coming to play with you. Remember my children would still be little kids, but you'd be a big boy. Why were you wondering?"

Joshua took another sip of his water. "Well, you know my father has more children now in his other house. And I hardly ever get to see him anymore. Why is that?"

Because your father must be a jerk, crossed my mind.

Chance cleared his throat. I could tell by his expression that his opinion of Joshua's father was the same as my own.

"Your father is very busy with his new family and all, but I'm sure he still thinks about you a lot. His children are still small and need a lot of attention. Once they get older, you'll probably start to see him more."

"I don't think Mom is very sure of that. She told me not to expect to see him around much anymore."

"Your mother probably was tired and said something she didn't exactly mean."

The boy gave him a dubious look.

"But look, even when your father can't be here, I can come by. We have fun together, don't we?"

Joshua nodded his head vigorously. Chance reached over and mussed his hair.

"And maybe we can go to a Red Sox game together this season, so you can see how the pros do it."

"Could we?"

"Sure, we'll even call your father and see if he can make it."

That would give Chance an opportunity to prod his former brother-in-law into taking his parental responsibilities seriously.

"But even if he can't go, we can still go, right?" Joshua said, proving that he knew the score.

"No matter what, we can still go," Chance reassured him.

"He's a nice kid," I said as we headed back to my place.

"In a tough situation."

"Most of us make it through and come out all right in the end."

Chance looked at me and nodded.

Chapter Twenty-Three

The phone rang and rang again, slowly bringing me up from a deep sleep. By the third ring, I looked at the clock and discovered it was only five-thirty-five. By the fourth ring, I reached over and answered it.

"Stormy!" a panicked voice cried.

"Yes. Who is this?"

"It's Maggie."

"What's wrong?" I asked, instantly alert.

"It's Ray! He's in the hospital. Somebody beat him up really bad. He's in a coma, and they're not sure whether he's ever going to wake up."

"Where is he?"

"At Ridley Hospital."

"Are you at the hospital now?"

"I'm outside intensive care. I couldn't make a call in there, but I'm standing right by the door. They called me because Ray had my name down as the one to contact in case of an emergency. I hate to ask this of you, but could you come down here and help me?"

Although not sure what help I could be, I understood why Maggie didn't want to face this alone.

"I'll be there in half an hour."

As soon as I hung up, I called Malone. He answered the phone sounding as if this were the middle of the day. How could he always be so awake? I explained about Ray being in the hospital, and Malone said he'd be by to pick me up in fifteen minutes.

I threw on my red sweater and jeans. It was cool enough out that I needed my leather jacket. I was ready in a few minutes and waited on the porch for Malone to arrive. He showed up right on the dot of fifteen minutes. When I got in the car, he had me repeat everything that Maggie had said.

"What do you know about Ray?" he asked me.

"Not much. You've met him. He always worked on having a bit of a bad boy image, but as far as I know, he didn't run with a violent crowd."

"He used drugs. It could have been a deal gone bad."

"Or it could have something to do with Mr. Adams."

Malone nodded.

We arrived at the hospital in ten minutes. We followed the arrows to intensive care. As we went through the sliding doors, there was a nurse's station immediately on our right. The nurse said that visiting time was restricted to fifteen minutes, and only two guests were allowed. Since Maggie was still there, Malone said he would wait outside.

I joined Maggie at Ray's bedside. He was barely recognizable. His head was wrapped in bandages, his left eye swollen shut, and his nose bent to one side. A deep abrasion ran down the side of his face.

"Oh, Stormy," Maggie said, hugging me tight. "They don't know if he's ever going to come around."

"What happened?"

"The police were asking the same thing, but I couldn't help them. Ray was found down near the river. It was just fortunate that someone happened to be walking by early in the morning coming home from a party. Who knows when he would have been discovered otherwise?"

Malone walked up and joined us.

"I talked the nurse into making an exception," he explained.

Once again, his amazing smile had gotten him around the rules.

He studied Ray in silence.

"Someone worked him over good."

"It's all my fault," said Maggie.

"What do you mean?" I asked.

"If only I'd gotten him to give up drugs, none of this would have happened."

"You think a drug dealer did this?" Chance asked.

"Who else?" Maggie said. "Ray was always short of cash. I loaned him some just a week ago. I warned him that was the last time. If only I hadn't been so hard-nosed. He probably owed some drug dealer money, and this was their way of punishing him."

"I thought Ray only used drugs occasionally," Malone said. "How deeply in debt could he be?"

"Who knows with that kind of thing," said Maggie.

Chance caught my eye, and I knew that his mind was following the same path as mine. It didn't lead to drug dealers.

"Do the police have any leads?"

Maggie shook her head. "They said they won't know anything until they can talk to Ray. But who knows when that will happen…if ever." Her eyes filled again with tears.

"Have you had anything to eat?" I asked.

"I can't eat."

"Well, let me at least get you a cup of coffee. I saw a machine as I was coming down the hall."

I nodded at Malone, and we walked out of intensive care together.

"What do you think?" I asked.

"It could have been drug dealers, I suppose."

"But you don't think so."

"If you hadn't told me about Ray talking to someone who looked like Adams' thug, I'd be more inclined to believe it."

"Why would Adams do this?"

"What if Ray promised he could get them the statues, then failed to do so? I can see them working him over. In fact, he's lucky to be alive."

I went up to the machine and fed it some money. We didn't say anything as the machine whirred and eventually filled the cup with inky liquid.

"How would Ray know where the statues are?" I asked.

"That's the question, isn't it? I should have talked to him sooner."

We went back to Ray's bedside. Maggie took a sip of the coffee and grimaced.

"I'm sure it's not very good," I said. "Machine coffee never is."

"It was nice of you to get it for me," Maggie said. "I have to go to the station to get things arranged for someone to replace Ray for this evening's broadcast. I'll come back to see him this afternoon."

"Who can you get to fill in on such short notice?" I asked.

"I'll ask Clarissa to take Sam away from Hildie until we can get a longer term replacement."

"Hildie won't be happy."

"She'll like it or lump it," Maggie snapped. "I'm tired of prima donnas like her making life hard for the rest of us who try to work as a team."

"I'm off this weekend. Maybe I could come in and give you a hand this afternoon?"

"That would be great."

"Remember orthoclase feldspar," I said.

"It's Ray who needs the luck," Maggie said with a faint smile.

As Malone and I walked across the parking lot to his car, he said, "What's this business about orthoclase feldspar?"

I explained about Maggie being a rock hound and how saying orthoclase feldspar had become our way of wishing the other person luck.

"Interesting," he said. "You know if what happened to Ray is some of Adams' work, it shows that he's getting more desperate."

"That means he might get tired of following you around town and use force to find out if you know more about the statues than you're telling."

"True," Malone said, but he was a beat too slow.

"You're also thinking that he might come after me if he suspects I killed Travis and took the statues," I said softly. The image of ending up like Ray or worse made me momentarily dizzy.

"It's a possibility. But I've been working on a plan for a couple of days to get Adams off the street before he can get to us. What happened to Ray gave me the last piece I needed."

"What are you going to do?"

"Give Adams what he wants, but I'll need a little

help from Lieutenant Green. There's also another piece to my plan. Are you still going out on your date with David tomorrow?"

"I told him I would."

"Good. Then there's something you can do for me."

Chapter Twenty-Four

I closed and locked the front door behind me. I was leaving for work in the late morning instead of waiting for the afternoon like I'd told Maggie. Since I'd been up since five-thirty, there'd been no getting back to sleep after I returned from the hospital. I'd completed all my chores and decided that I might as well help Maggie deal with her understaffed situation. I was no cameraman, but there were things I'd picked up along the way with regard to the computers that might allow me to lessen her burden.

I was unlocking my car door when something was pulled over my head. Before I even had a chance to struggle, I was off my feet and being carried away. I shouted and screamed, but whatever was over my head muffled the sound. A few seconds later, I was tossed onto something soft and heard a door slam behind me. I immediately pulled the covering from over my head and saw it was a rather dirty looking blanket. Sitting across from me in the back of the limo was Mr. Adams. I twisted around looking for a way to escape, but up front, the thug had gotten behind the wheel, and the car was already pulling away from the curb.

Adams' sunglass-covered eyes were fixed on me.

"I apologize for our heavy-handed way of getting you to come on this little trip. But I doubted that you would join us willingly."

"Where are you taking me? This is kidnapping."

I reached over and tried to open the door. Even though the car was picking up speed, I might have been desperate enough to jump out.

"The doors are all locked, Ms. McCloud. There is no need for you to be alarmed. We are merely going to a house I have leased so we can have a conversation about the location of my property."

I sank back in the seat and tried to regain my composure, which wasn't easy since images of Ray kept running through my head. I figured he'd recently had a *conversation* with Mr. Adams. I thought of what my father had once told me, that when I found myself in a stressful situation, it was important to stay calm and think it through. Good advice, hard to implement.

"I know nothing about your property."

"I hope for your sake that isn't true. Because I can become very irritable when I don't get what I want."

"Is that what happened to Ray?"

"Ah, that was a special case. Ray promised to deliver my merchandise to me then failed to do so. However, I did learn something important from that young man."

"What?" I asked reluctantly.

"I found out that my property, at least until a day ago, was on the grounds of your television station."

"I don't know anything about that."

"But you see that is most unlikely. Mr. Lambert died by your house and my property disappeared. Now it turns up at the television station where you work. I'm afraid the most likely scenario is that you killed Mr. Lambert and took my merchandise."

"I didn't do either one."

"Perhaps you are telling the truth, perhaps not. To find out which is the case, I'm afraid I will have to resort to more intense questioning."

"It won't help. I don't know anything."

"If that is true, let me express my sorrow in advance for what I must do."

I sat back and tried to keep my lips from trembling. The only way to remain relatively calm was to watch where I was being taken. I already had the vague impression that we were heading west into the Berkshires. In fifteen minutes, we would be in the rural countryside where houses were so far apart that no one would be aware of what their neighbor was doing, even if it led to screaming. I pushed that away and calculated my odds of being rescued. In a few hours, I'd be missed at work if Maggie remembered that I'd promised to come in. That might just possibly lead to a call to the police or to Malone, but by that time the damage would be done. I could tell Adams where one of his statues was, Malone had told me he'd locked it in his office safe. But I didn't think Adams was going to be satisfied with one out of ten. It might just make him more aggressive in torturing me. I decided the best policy was to claim complete ignorance for as long as I could.

We turned off the paved road onto a gravel drive. The trees were close enough to the sides of the drive that they brushed against the limousine. After what seemed to be a long time, but was probably only a couple of minutes, we pulled into a circular driveway in front of what looked very much like an Alpine ski chateau.

"Welcome to my temporary home away from home," Adams said with a faint smile.

The car came to a stop. The thug who was driving opened the door, grabbed my arm tightly, and pulled me out of the car. He waited for Adams to precede him, then he tugged on my arm, and half-dragged me up to the front door. Adams opened the door, and my escort pulled me into a large room to the right of the front door. It was over decorated but shabby. Furniture seemed to fill every available nook and cranny, but most of it looked the worse for wear.

A straight-backed wooden chair stood in the center of the room. I was forced to sit there. As I watched with growing fear of what was going to happen next, the two men arranged themselves around the room. The chauffeur, who had cold, light blue eyes, stood directly in front of me. Adams moved to my extreme left and leaned against the front of a desk.

"Now that you've had some time to consider the situation, Ms. McCloud, are you ready to tell me the whereabouts of my property?"

"I'm afraid that I still don't know where your property is."

I tried to sound firm and reasonable but my voice was a little high, and it shook.

"Before we begin, perhaps you should tape her wrists together," Adams said.

The chauffeur took a roll of gray duct tape off of an end table and approached me. As he moved toward me, I saw that he wore a gun on his left side.

"Stand up," he ordered.

I got to my feet.

I wouldn't have been able to do what I did next if I'd had time to think about it. But once my hands were bound, it would be all over.

"Turn around."

I started to turn but then pretended to stumble toward him. He automatically reached out with his empty right hand to steady me. As I stumbled I twisted to my right and pulled the gun out of his holster, then I took a quick step backwards, knocking over the chair. Recognizing it by feel alone, I thanked my lucky stars that he was carrying another Glock.

He took a step toward me, but something in my face caused him to stop. I glanced over at Adams, but he kept his hands at his sides. I hoped he was unarmed.

"Don't be silly, Ms. McCloud. This will only make things worse," Adams said.

He nodded toward the chauffeur, who reluctantly moved toward me.

The vase on the table next to his right arm exploded into fragments. He jumped to his left. Then he looked at his right hand, which had begun to bleed.

"Another step and I start aiming at people," I said.

The thug was watching me intently. His hands remained loose at his sides, but there was fury in his eyes. He wouldn't underestimate me again.

"Stay right where you are," I warned him.

I could see him debating whether to obey, measuring distances in his mind. I kept my gun trained on the center of his chest. I didn't know whether I'd have the nerve to shoot or not, but I wanted to appear as if I would.

I glanced over at Adams, who didn't appear to be a threat.

"Take one step and I shoot your boss," I told the thug, pointing my gun at the center of Adams' chest.

"You wouldn't shoot an unarmed man," Adams

said.

"Do you really want to find out?"

Adams stared hard at me for a moment. "Stay where you are," he ordered the chauffeur.

I walked carefully around the thug, keeping at a safe distance. I slowly backed out of the room. Both men remained frozen in place.

I continued walking backwards out the front door and almost bumped into the limousine. I was about to check whether the keys were in the ignition when a voice from the other side of the limousine said, "Stormy?"

I looked up, and Malone was coming around the car toward me. He was carrying a gun.

"My car is a few yards down the road. Let's go," he said. He quickly put a bullet in each of the rear tires of the limo.

We had left the gravel and turned onto the road before Malone spoke to me again. He had been focused on the rear view mirror, and I was feeling too exhausted to talk.

"I heard a shot back there. What happened?"

I explained. I felt like I was talking in slow motion, it took so long for each word to reach the surface.

Malone gave my shoulder a squeeze.

"Good work. I was keeping an eye on your house. But I was too far away to do anything when they snatched you, so I tailed them, hoping I'd get a chance to rescue you."

I nodded. "Where are we going now?"

"We're going to go to the television station if you still feel up to helping there. You'll be safer at the station than alone at home."

"And I can't leave Maggie even more in the lurch than she already is."

"I have to meet with Lieutenant Green, but give me a call when you're ready to leave."

"I can't have you following me around forever," I said.

"You won't have to. This case is coming to a conclusion. Hopefully, by tomorrow night it will all be over. Don't forget what you have to do tomorrow."

"What about tomorrow?"

"Tomorrow you have your date with David."

"Will it be safe?" I asked. The only thing I could think about at the moment was safety.

"If my plan works, Adams will have lost interest in you by then."

"Okay, but under one condition.

"What's that?"

I picked the Glock off the seat between us. I had placed it there next to me like a friendly traveling companion. I tucked it in the waistband of my slacks.

"You can't carry a gun around like that."

"I'll grab my purse when I get home and put it in there."

"It's still illegal."

"Right now, I don't care."

Malone studied my face then kept quiet.

****

We followed Malone's plan, and I went to the station. Working on autopilot, I somehow managed to get through the day's responsibilities. When I was at my busiest, I could almost forget what had happened to me that morning. Once things slowed down, it would come rushing back with the emotional force of a

226

nightmare. I would sit at my desk, very still, until the trembling stopped. I kept imagining that Adams and his thug would come through the station door any minute, so I kept my purse with the gun at my side. When the day was finally over, I called Malone, and he met me at the door.

"Any sign of Adams or his men?" I asked as we walked across the parking lot.

Malone shook his head. "No, and I haven't been followed all day. But I called Adams earlier at the number that was on the business card he gave me."

"You called *him!*"

"It's part of my plan to get him off the street. I'm going to help him break into the television station tomorrow night."

"How is that going to make us any better off?"

"I've already worked out an arrangement with Lieutenant Green. He'll be waiting and arrest them once they're inside."

"What will he charge them with?"

"Breaking and entering; kidnapping you; the attack on Ray, we'll have to see what sticks. At least it will get them off the streets. If we don't do that, Adams is going to keep coming after us."

"And he wants to break into the station because he thinks that's where the statues are?"

"Ray claimed they were there."

"But when push came to shove he couldn't produce them, and who brought them to the station in the first place?"

"The person who killed Travis."

"Who is that?"

"I'm not sure yet."

"So is Adams going to search the entire station?"

"No. I told him that I know where the statues are."

"Do you?"

"No. But hopefully Green will have sprung his trap before Adams finds that out."

"Sounds very risky."

"There's some risk. But the police will provide lots of backup."

"And you still want me to go on my date with David?"

"That's an essential part of the plan."

"Where are we going now?"

"Since we don't have to worry about Adams causing us any more trouble, for the time being, I'll drive you home. You can spend the night there. Go to your lunch tomorrow with David, and give me a call on my cell somewhere along the way to let me know how it's going."

"That's all I have to do?"

"Yes, but it's an important part. Okay?"

I nodded but didn't like the feeling that I was being kept in the dark about an essential part of the plan.

Chapter Twenty-Five

I had to admit that the Wagon Wheel Inn knew how to put on a brunch. A whole table was devoted to rolls, bagels, pastries, and teacakes. There were a variety of fruits, hot cereal, cold cereal, and eggs Benedict. A chef even stood ready to make an omelet how ever you wanted it. Another table held a wide assortment of breakfast meats in addition to roast beef, turkey, and an array of cheeses. It was all a bit overwhelming. Maybe some people found this to be the solution to their giant appetites, but for me, currently having little or no appetite at all due to nerves, it was simply too much from which to choose. Finally, I decided on a cheese omelet, a small raspberry pastry, a piece of turkey on a small roll, and a cup of coffee.

"Is that all you're going to have?" David asked, returning to the table with a heaping plateful of food.

"For right now, anyway," I said. "How do you stay so slender when you eat like that?"

"A fast metabolism," David replied with a smile. "I've always been able to eat pretty much whatever I want and not gain weight. I wasn't sure I'd be able to continue doing it as I got older, but so far I have."

"Do you get a lot of exercise?"

"Nothing special. On nice days, I walk to the college. That's about a mile each way. Other than that I'm too busy to set aside time for exercise what with teaching a full course load and being director of the gallery."

"I can imagine."

"Fortunately, I'm on sabbatical this semester, so I only have the gallery to worry about."

"What are you doing with your free time?"

"Working on a book on a minor Dutch painter."

"Sounds interesting."

David shrugged. "Only if you're in the field. What do you do for exercise?"

"I belong to a gym that I don't get to as often as I'd like, and I take yoga classes."

"I hear that's good for flexibility."

"It's also a good way to relax. I've really needed that lately."

"Being the suspect in a murder investigation must be very trying."

"There's actually more than that going on. Ray, one of our cameramen, was badly beaten last night."

"That's too bad. Does anyone know why?"

"Some people think it had to do with drugs, but Malone thinks otherwise."

I paused to take a bite from the delicious whole grain roll.

"What does Malone think?"

"He thinks Ray tried to make a deal with some criminals to sell them the statues."

David looked up from his plate in surprise. "Where did he come up with that idea?"

"Actually, he's got a pretty convincing argument. Let's see if I can remember exactly what he said." I paused as if to think, although I had memorized exactly what to say. "First of all, there's the question of where

Travis could have hidden the statues. They weren't in his apartment, and they weren't in my basement with his drug stash."

"He stashed drugs in your basement?" David asked, startled.

I explained what we'd found and about the attack on Bud McDonald.

"That's terrible. So Travis had a key to your basement and was using it without your knowledge."

I nodded. "I know, it's hard to believe, and very disturbing."

"But you said that the statues weren't found there?"

"No, only drugs. So Malone thinks that the only other place Travis went regularly and where he might have hidden them is the television station."

"Where at the station?"

"Well, the logical place would be in his desk. He was very private about that."

"But surely someone has gone through his desk by now."

"I was there when the police looked around. They checked his appointment book and opened the drawers and poked around a little. But nobody actually *searched* his desk. Malone thinks something could be hidden out of sight."

"Has he taken a look yet?"

I shook my head. "He needs to get permission from Mr. Harris first. Malone is going to see him the first thing tomorrow morning."

"What was Travis doing with the statues?"

I explained about the drug deal and Travis' attempt to strike a bargain with Adams. When David asked me how I knew all this, I claimed that Malone had gotten it from a confidential source.

"So, Travis tried selling the statues back to the thief who had transported them to this country. Sounds like a dangerous game," David said.

"Malone thinks that's what got Travis killed. He tried to double-cross the thieves."

"But the thieves never got the statues?"

"Apparently not, because they're still around looking for them."

David smiled. "This is all very exciting. Just like a crime novel."

"It's a lot more fun reading about it than living through it."

David reached across the table and touched the back of my hand. "I invited you out to take your mind off of your troubles, and here I am making you dwell on them. That wasn't what I intended. Although I will admit it's all very fascinating."

"That's okay. In fact, it's been rather cathartic to talk about all of this with somebody new. Do you think Malone's idea makes sense?"

"Well, he's making a number of assumptions that could be wrong, but it certainly seems worth following up on. After all, there don't seem to be many other good ideas out there."

I nodded. "I'm just worried that someone has already figured this all out and has already searched Travis' desk and gotten the statues."

"I would think that with people around your offices all the time. It wouldn't be easy for a stranger to just walk in and start searching."

"Not during the day, but after midnight the place is

pretty much just locked up and left. There isn't any security guard and the station is remote out there on top of the mountain."

"But surely there's a security system?"

I nodded and dropped my voice to a whisper. "Don't tell anybody, but it hasn't worked for the last month. The security guy says he needs a part that isn't easy to get."

"I still think you're worrying about nothing," David said. "What are the odds that someone is going to break in between twelve o'clock tonight and tomorrow morning when Malone searches the desk?"

"I guess the odds are pretty small. But I've been so spooked lately with everything that's been going on, I keep imagining the worst things that could happen."

David smiled. "Well, nothing gets your mind off crime as quickly as art."

After talking about art for the rest of the meal, David suggested we should leave. I excused myself to go to the ladies' room. After checking to see that it was empty, I took out my cell phone and punched in Malone's number.

"How'd it go?" he asked.

"Well, I did what you told me, but I'm still skeptical."

"I talked with Adams again this morning to firm up the arrangements. He's going to pick me up in front of my office at midnight."

"Did Mr. Harris go along with your plan?"

"A little reluctantly. I don't think he was very happy about the possible damage a break-in would cause. I reassured him that it would be confined to the back door, which has a simple lock and can be pried open easily with a crowbar. I'll tell Adams about that so he doesn't do more damage than he has to."

"And Lieutenant Green is all ready?"

"He's still not too happy that we didn't tell him about Adams earlier, but he's going along with the trap."

Another woman came into the ladies' room, and I had to whisper. "How did you explain your knowledge of the statues to Green?"

"I said that Adams had told me about them."

"You didn't say we found one."

"No, I'd rather we didn't have to admit to that just yet."

"We may not be able to avoid it."

"I know. But we'll see how things play out. I convinced Lieutenant Green to let you come along with him tonight as long as you stay out of the way. Meet him at the station at eleven o'clock."

"It must have been hard to convince him to allow me along."

"Yeah, I pretty much had to make it a precondition of my doing it at all. But I thought you'd earned the right to be there at the end."

"Did you say anything about David to him?"

"No, I just warned him not to be too quick to spring the trap. We'll just have to see what happens."

"You really think David could be involved in all this?"

"Someone knocked out Bud with a stun gun. I don't think it was Adams, and who else knew about the statues?"

"I suppose. Also, David just told me he's on sabbatical this semester so he would have had the free time to follow me around."

"That makes me suspect him even more."

I wondered whether Malone might be letting jealousy cloud his judgment, but didn't say anything.

"Are you going to be wearing a microphone or some high tech gadget tonight so the police know when to make their move?"

Malone paused before he answered. "Too risky. Odds are I'll be searched. No, I told Green to give me fifteen minutes inside and then make their move. I figured I could delay things that long if I'm lucky."

"So Adams isn't letting you take your own car?"

"No, he insisted that we travel together. He said it would be more collegial. I figured it was a way to make it harder for me to get away if things went wrong."

There was a moment of silence. I should get back to David, who would be wondering what had happened to me.

Finally, I said, "Well, good luck. I'm sure this will go just as we planned."

"Things like this never go the way they're planned, but I hope it turns out all right."

Chapter Twenty-Six

I stood hidden in the shadows near the front of Chance's office building. He didn't know I was there and wouldn't have been happy if he did. I watched him pull his jacket closer around him. It must have been nerves bothering him rather than the cold because it was warm for an April night. He was waiting for Adams. Chance had said things always went wrong. That's why I was there. If things went wrong, I planned to be on the scene with my Glock to set them right. Chance was risking his life for me, and that went beyond his obligations as a private investigator. He was doing it because he cared for me, and I was determined to prove that I cared for him as well.

I wondered if Chance was praying right now, and whether God would hear his prayer. Maybe He had, maybe that's why I was there. The thought of being an agent of God made me want to laugh or cry. I wasn't sure which. I just knew I wasn't going to allow Chance to risk his life while I waited in safety with the police. We'd been in this together from the start. We were a team. We'd been together each step along the way, and I planned to carry that out until the end.

A dark car came down the street and stopped in front of Chance. By the light of the streetlamp, I saw the thug get out from behind the wheel. He made Chance put his hands on the hood and thoroughly patted him down. It gave me a secret rush of power to be so close and yet unobserved. I could understand the desire people have always had to be invisible.

"Since we're on the same side now, maybe I should have a name to call you." Chance said.

"Call me Michael—never Mike—only Michael."

Michael opened the rear door, and Chance slid inside. Across from him, I imagined Adams, or whatever his real name was, sitting. Before the door closed, I heard him speak.

"Ah, so we meet again, Mr. Malone. And this time, you know the location of my property."

"It's just an educated guess."

"I hope for your sake it is a correct one."

The door slammed shut, cutting off their voices.

I slipped down the alley behind me that led to the back parking lot and my car. I knew a shortcut to the station that should get me there ahead of Chance and Adams. Keeping to just within the speed limit, I arrived in ten minutes. I pulled my car well back among the trees. The police wouldn't have arrived early because they didn't want to spook Adams, so no one was there to observe me. I moved across the parking lot, staying away from the lights and hiding in the shadows as much as I could. Even though I was reasonably certain no one was around watching, I didn't want to be more conspicuous that I had to be.

I used my key to get in through the front door. Using a flashlight, I made my way over to my desk and partially opened the window. This faced out on the back parking lot where Chance would direct Adams to park. As soon as they got inside, I'd slip into a nearby closet where I could see and hear what was happening without being spotted. About five minutes later I heard the limousine pull up behind the station.

When all the men were out of the car, I heard Michael say, "What if the cops check around the back of the building?"

"Every plan has its risks," Chance answered. "But we won't be here long."

"Let us hope not," Mr. Adams said.

Michael walked up to the back door of the building. There was the squealing sound of screws being forced out of wood.

"The door's open," Michael announced.

"Shall we go in then?" Adams said as if the announcement had been made that dinner was served.

Once they were inside, Chance had to spend at least fifteen minutes in a convincing imitation of a search before the police would spring their trap. I quickly closed the window and went into the closet, keeping the door ajar. Chance led the way into the bullpen, setting an intentionally slow pace. Since the only window looked out on the parking lot, Adams ordered Michael to turn on the lights. I pulled my door slightly more closed.

"Ah, that's better," said Adams. He turned to Chance. "Now which desk belonged to Travis Lambert?"

Chance stood for a moment, apparently thinking.

"Come, come, don't waste my time," snapped Adams.

"That one over by the window," Chance replied.

"Ah, how droll, they put the weatherman by the window." He looked at Chance. "I would suggest that you start looking and pray that you find something."

Chance approached the desk and pulled open the middle drawer. He removed the drawer and dumped it out on top of the desk. All it held were pencils and pens. He turned the drawer over to see if anything was attached to the bottom.

"Wouldn't he have locked the desk if something so valuable were in it?" Adams asked.

"The police unlocked it, but they did only a cursory search." Chance stared at the desk as if it might reveal its secrets just by looking.

"Move on," Adams barked.

Chance tried the first drawer on the right. He searched all around inside for something that might be taped under the desktop but to no avail. He removed that drawer as well and emptied out the maps and office supplies, so he could examine the bottom.

"Move more quickly, Mr. Malone. This isn't looking very promising."

Chance took out the bottom drawer on the right. Again, he examined the inside of the opening carefully, then went on to empty the drawer—again, nothing. Chance moved to the left-hand side of the desk. He risked a glance at his watch. I knew only five long minutes had passed, still ten minutes to kill before the cavalry arrived. If the desk proved to be empty, as it doubtlessly would, Adams might order Michael to shoot Chance on the spot. That would bring the police running, but too late. I slipped the Glock out of my jacket pocket and moved my legs a little to make sure they hadn't fallen asleep.

Chance opened the first drawer on the left side. All it had inside was an appointment book and some sheets of paper. He made a great show of examining everything carefully.

"More quickly, Mr. Malone, or I will have Michael subdue you and take over the search myself."

Chance glanced over his shoulder. I could see that Michael had his gun out and pointed in Chance's direction. If it came to a shootout, I figured I had the advantage of surprise. I was pretty good at hitting targets, but I wasn't sure how I'd be at shooting a man. I figured that was something I'd never know until the time came.

Chance opened the next drawer and took out a rectangular package wrapped in brown paper.

"That looks more promising," Adams said, smiling. "Perhaps you have been vindicated, after all, Mr. Malone. Please bring the package to me."

Chance had taken two steps toward Adams when Michael gave a loud grunt and fell to the floor. Behind him appeared a smaller man wearing a ski mask. He now held Michael's gun in one hand and a stun gun in the other.

"Please ignore that earlier order," he said to Chance in an artificially high voice. "Bring the package to me."

"You are making a serious mistake," Adams said, his hand starting for the inside of his coat.

"Don't do that," the stranger said, pointing Michael's gun in Adams' direction. "I don't want to shoot anyone, but I will if I have to."

Chance changed direction and moved slowly toward the man with the ski mask, trying to kill time because the police should be arriving any minute.

"Put it down on the desk and back away," the man ordered when Chance was within five feet. Chance did as he was told. He slowly took four steps back.

The man put the stun gun down on the desk and walked forward slowly, keeping Michael's gun pointed midway between Chance and Adams. He picked up the package.

"I'm going to leave now. Don't try to follow me."

"I wouldn't dream of it," Chance said. "And remember the old saying, sometimes a cigar is only a cigar."

The masked man stopped as if puzzled. Then, keeping the gun in one hand, he used the other to slowly tear the brown paper off the box. It was an awkward process since he had to keep looking up to check on the positions of Adams and Chance while balancing the box. Finally the last of the brown paper fell to the floor. He opened the box.

"It's a box of cigars," he said, amazed.

"You tried to cheat me," Adams shouted at Chance.

He fumbled under his coat and came up with a gun, but by then I had charged out of the closet. I fired one quick shot and was surprised when Adams fell. The man in the mask seemed to have been left a beat behind by the action. When he finally turned toward me, I had already pointed the gun at the center of his chest.

"Put down the gun," I shouted, half-deafened by the gunshot.

Before he could respond, there was a series of loud shouts and cops seemed to appear from everywhere. The man in the mask dropped his gun and put his hands high in the air. I immediately put my gun down on my official weather desk, not wanting to risk becoming collateral damage.

"What are you doing here?" Chance said, coming toward me. I could tell that he wasn't sure whether to be angry or amazed. I began to shake, probably a reaction to shooting a man.

"Keeping an eye on you," I said softly.

I don't know whether it was the adrenaline or happiness at being alive, but I wrapped my arms around him and kissed him hard on the lips. After a surprised moment, he began to respond.

"Are you okay?" I whispered in his ear when I was done.

"I'm fine. Thanks to you."

"I figured you could handle it, but I wasn't sure Lieutenant Green would get here on time."

"He didn't. Not really. Once again I owe you my life. I think that means we belong together."

I looked into his eyes to see if he was serious. There was nothing to give me any cause to doubt.

"I think you're right," I replied.

Lieutenant Green entered the room and began shouting orders.

"Am I going to be in big trouble for shooting Mr. Adams with an unregistered gun?" I asked.

"I have a feeling that Green is going to be willing to let you off with a reprimand under the circumstances."

Chance looked over in the direction of the masked man. The mask was now off, and David was adamantly refusing to say anything until he had seen his lawyer.

"We were lucky he came along when he did," Chance said. "He put Michael out of commission and killed time opening the box. If Adams had opened that box with Michael at his side, things would have gotten ugly real fast."

Chance and I walked over to David. He was still staring at the box of cigars.

"You put those there," David said in an accusing voice to Chance.

"Guilty as charged."

"You never had the statues?" he asked.

Chance shook his head. "I have no idea where they are."

David looked at me reproachfully. "You tricked me."

"And I'm sure your sudden interest in me had more to do with the statues than my personality."

David gave me a lingering look. "We'll never know the truth about that now, will we?"

As the police led David away along with a still groggy Michael, the EMTs were working over Adams. I walked over.

"Will he make it?" I asked.

"He'll be fine. It's only a shoulder wound," one of them told me. "He'll be sore for a while, but he'll be in great shape for his trial."

Since I'd aimed for his heart, I figured I wasn't as good a shot as I thought I was. I said a small prayer of thanks for that and wondered if this religious stuff was starting to rub off on me. I walked over to where Chance was standing by Travis' desk."

"Your search of that desk was quite the striptease. You dragged it out longer than I thought possible. You went though almost all the drawers."

"All except this bottom one," Chance said, casually, reaching down and pulling it open. He stared inside for a moment, and then quickly shut it. "The statues are in there," he whispered.

I laughed. "Very funny."

"I'm not kidding."

I looked around to make certain that the police were otherwise occupied. Slowly I slid the drawer open. Sure enough, there was an open wooden box filled with straw, and staring up at me in all their fierceness were nine little figures. There was even an indentation in the straw where the tenth figure had been.

"So your lie turned out not to be a lie after all. Maybe God made it come true," I said, almost half-believing what I was saying.

"I'm not sure He does favors like that."

"What are we going to do? We have to tell the police."

"Just a minute," Chance whispered. He reached in his pocket and took out the statue of Indra, the god of storms. "I brought this with me in case I had to prove to Adams at the last desperate moment that I knew where the statues were."

Quickly, he dropped it in the last slot and closed the drawer.

"What do we do next?" I asked.

"Now we make Lieutenant Green a very happy man."

Chapter Twenty-Seven

The next day I was sitting in the break room in the middle of the afternoon when Chance walked in. I'd been pretty much out of it all day, wondering what was going on at the police station and if I was really going to be off the hook. I found myself grinning from ear to ear as he came over to my table. Remembering how worried I had been about him last night and how happy I was to see him today convinced me that my feelings for Chance were deeper than I had believed possible.

"Any sign that the folks around here have heard about what happened last night?" he asked softly.

"A couple of people noticed that the back door had been damaged. Mr. Harris blamed it on mindless vandalism. Otherwise, there hasn't been a peep."

"Good. I know Lieutenant Green talked to his guys about keeping a lid on it for today. Mr. Harris should be the only one who knows here, and he promised not to tell anyone, not even that station manager."

"I guess everyone has been as good as their word because it's been positively boring. What's been happening with you since last night?"

"I spent most of the night and part of the morning talking to the police. Do you want an update?"

"Of course."

"Well, first of all, our friend David Palmer is claiming that he was trying to retrieve the statues from the thieves, so he could turn them over to the FBI. He was working as a sort of one man justice squad."

"Do you think that's likely?"

"Considering he never contacted the FBI in the first place like he told you, I doubt it."

"Why did he lie to me?"

"He was probably hoping that if we had all the statues, he could frighten us into turning them all over to him. He'd sell them and tell us he gave them to the FBI. We'd never know otherwise."

"So he was lying to us all along?"

"From the very start. One thing he did admit to the police is that he knew about the statues long before we showed Indra to him. He and Travis were friends, so when the items came into Travis' possession, he showed them to David to try to find out how much they were worth. David claims that Travis never told him they were stolen. My bet is that he knew all along, and Travis promised him a cut of the take."

"So he was just pretending to see the statue for the first time when we went to his office?"

"Right. In fact, I'd venture to say that he called to see if you were all right the day the body was discovered because he wanted to get close to you and find out if you had the statues. When we brought him the Indra, he was pretty well convinced that we knew where they all were. That's why he was following you and saw you visit Bud Macdonald. He followed Bud to your house and used the stun gun on him so he could search the basement."

"Are they going to be able to charge him with the attack on Bud?"

"Hard to tell. According to Green, Bud is starting

to remember what happened a little more clearly, and apparently, David wasn't wearing a ski mask when he attacked him because Bud remembers seeing a face. They're going to see if Bud can pick David out of a lineup later today. For right now, they've got David dead to rights for possession of a stun gun, and I'll bet Green is thinking up more charges as we speak. I don't know how much jail time he'll do, but his career at the college is probably over."

And there goes the nice, stable guy I thought would be perfect for me. There were a lot of things I'd liked about David, but I was surprised to find that I didn't have any regrets. He had played me, and that was something I wouldn't forgive.

"What will happen to Adams and his thug?"

"Well, Adams came through the surgery just fine. That's the end of the good news for him. They've got him for breaking and entering, the attack on you, and I heard through the grapevine that the Boston police are anxious to talk to him about a couple of art thefts. Did you know that Ray is out of intensive care?"

"Yes. Maggie told me this morning."

"Well, with any luck, he should be able to identify Michael as the one who attacked him. In addition to any jail time Adams does, he's also out the cost of his property. Green already contacted the FBI, and they're taking charge of the statues until they're needed at trial."

I paused for a moment. "Somehow it seems that everyone is getting off rather easily here. As much as I didn't like him, Travis was murdered. Somebody should have to pay for that."

"Lieutenant Green figures that Michael probably

did it. He and Adams followed Travis to your house that night with the intention of getting the statues back without paying Travis. But Michael jumped the gun and killed him before Travis got them from his hiding place."

"Then how did the statues disappear from my basement and end up at the station?"

Chance smiled. "Green doesn't have that quite worked out yet. I think he figures that Travis had them hidden at the station all along, and somehow they were overlooked by the police search of his desk."

"But why didn't Adams and Michael break into my basement at the same time they killed Travis?"

"Green thinks they got there too soon to see where he was heading. They saw him walk around the side of your house and chased him. When he refused to divulge where he had hidden the statues, Michael hit him a little too hard."

"With a rock? Somehow that doesn't sound like Michael's style. Like you said from the first, wouldn't he have worked him over with his fists or a gun butt? Something more professional."

"I didn't say Green's theory was perfect. But it's the one he's pushing ahead with."

"At least it gets me off the hook, but I wish I found it more convincing."

Chance paused and gave me a long, speculative look. I could see that he was reluctant to speak.

"What are you thinking?"

"A new piece of evidence has given me an alternative theory, but you're not going to like it."

"As you would say, if it's the truth, I'll have to accept it. Tell me what you've got."

When Chance got done explaining his theory, I looked at him grimly.

"That can't be. You must be wrong."

"You're smart. If you think about it, there's only one way this could have happened."

"What are you going to do?" I finally asked.

"You know what I would do. But this one is up to you."

****

I had just finished my afternoon weather update. Sam, who was still working as Ray's replacement despite Hildie's strong objection that she couldn't function without her right hand man, hurried down to the break room leaving Maggie and me alone in the studio. Speaking in a low voice, just in case the studio walls had ears, I told her quickly and concisely about the status of the case.

Maggie's face broke into a broad smile. "So it looks like you're off the hook on the murder charge," she said, giving me a big hug.

"It does," I said taking a step back.

"I just hope the Lieutenant can make the charges stick against this Adams guy. People like that always seem to get away with things."

"Oh, I'm pretty sure Green will do his best to convict Adams of Travis' murder," I assured her.

"Good."

"Of course, we both know that Adams had nothing to do with Travis' death."

Maggie gave me a puzzled smile. "What do you mean?"

"I mean we both know that you killed Travis."

A doubtful smile played across Maggie's lips.

"That's not funny, Stormy."

"It wasn't meant to be."

"Why would I want to kill Travis? I hardly knew him."

"That's not quite true either, is it? You and Travis were lovers. On Monday you heard that Travis was involved with Debbie. It had been a secret up until then because Travis didn't want you to know. What had he promised you, that you were the only one, and he'd be faithful to you?"

Maggie was quiet for a moment and then gave a bitter laugh. "Pretty much. He said that he'd run around a lot in the past, but now that he had me, someone who would look out for him, he didn't need anyone else. I was helping him make demo tapes so he could get into a bigger market. He kept telling me how we'd go to Boston, and both get to work at a large station. And I believed him. Me—everyone's mother, but nobody's girlfriend. I thought that had finally changed. When I heard about Debbie, I realized I had just been fooling myself."

"What happened that night?"

"I went to his apartment but saw him driving away just as I got there. So I followed him to your place. I didn't know that was where you lived, or I never would have buried his body there. You have to believe that."

"Oh, I think you knew. You thought Travis and I were having an affair, so why shouldn't I take the blame for his death."

Maggie was silent for a moment. "Now I know that wasn't true. I'm sorry."

"What did Travis do when he got to my house?"

"He parked about a block away, and I followed

him as he slinked up to your place. I was a little way behind him when he went around the back. When I turned the corner of the house, he'd disappeared. I was about to peek in the window to see if he was inside when he came up from the basement, surprising us both."

"'What are you doing here?' he said to me. Like I was an annoyance that he wanted to get out of his life. It got me so angry that all my accusations came pouring out. He said he didn't have time to deal with me right then, and he'd explain things in the morning. Then he brushed past me like I was a big, fat obstacle in his way. So I picked up a rock, ran after him, and hit him on the head. I was so angry. But I don't think I actually meant to kill him. When I saw he was dead, I didn't know what to do. All I could think of was to hide his body right away. I always carry a small shovel in my car for rock hunting, so I used it to bury him in a shallow grave. I made so much noise that I thought at any moment someone was going to investigate and see me. I planned on coming back the next night and moving him somewhere where he'd never be found. I really wasn't trying to get you in trouble."

"But Bud decided to build a garage on that spot the next morning."

Maggie nodded with a sad smile. "Just my luck. But you have to believe me, I never intended to get you involved in this whole thing. I didn't know what else to do. I never would have let you go to jail. I would have confessed first."

So many people had been lying lately, that I didn't know whether to believe her or not. From the expression on Maggie's face, however, I thought she might be telling the truth.

"What about the statues?"

"He had the box in his hand when I hit him, and they scattered everywhere. Fortunately, I had a flashlight in the car, so I picked up as many as I could find. I took them with me. I don't really know why. I just didn't want to leave behind anything that was a clue."

"And you brought them back to the station."

Maggie nodded at a battered desk in the far corner of the studio. "I put them there. We never use that desk, so I figured they'd be safe there until I decided what to do with them. I didn't know they were valuable or I'd have gotten rid of them right away."

"But Ray found them?"

"I was here. I saw him happen to open the drawer one day looking for something. I didn't think he even knew what they were, but I couldn't take the risk. I moved them to Travis' desk because if they were found there, no one would associate them with me. The only one who could link them to me was Ray, and he wouldn't squeal. How did Ray know what the statues were?"

"Adams told him. He was working as Adams' inside man."

"So that's why he got beat up. Ray told Adams he knew where they were. When I switched them, it put Ray on the spot." Tears came into Maggie's eyes. "Once more I got someone I love hurt."

"So you put them in the desk Friday night, right after our last newscast?"

Maggie nodded.

"Chance didn't see them on Sunday when he

slipped cigars in the desk because he never looked in the bottom drawer."

"How did you figure out it was me?"

"I didn't. Chance found a birthday card that Travis had left in his apartment. There was a note in it about his taking someone out to Deming, New Mexico. Chance did a little research and found that Deming is a major place where rock hounds go. So when I explained to him in the hospital about our little joke about orthoclase feldspar and how rock collecting was your hobby, he put two and two together."

Maggie's eyes filled with tears. "So Travis really did plan to take me on vacation for my birthday. He promised me, but I didn't believe him. That proves he loved me in some small way."

"I'm sure he did." In some small way, I added to myself.

"What happens now?" Maggie asked, drying her eyes and suddenly all business.

"Chance is waiting out in the bullpen to take you down to the police station. He's already arranged for a good criminal lawyer to meet you there. Turning yourself in voluntarily will help your case."

Maggie slowly got to her feet like she'd aged forty years. She stumbled a little, and I took her arm. As I opened the studio door, I whispered for the last time "orthoclase feldspar."

"And the same to you, Stormy," Maggie replied. "The same to you."

Chapter Twenty-Eight

Chance turned in the driveway of the restaurant. The ornate plaque that hung above the door was of a deer running across one quadrant of a coat of arms.

"I've always wondered why this restaurant is called the Golden Hind," I said. "I heard somewhere that the Golden Hind was an old sailing ship."

"That's right. The one Sir Francis Drake sailed around the world on in the 16th century."

I stared at him. "How do you know that?"

He shrugged. "History is sort of a hobby of mine."

I thought how little I knew about this man that I had decided I loved. But somehow I felt I knew enough, at least about the important things.

"Then why the picture of the deer?"

"Apparently the original name of Drake's ship was the Pelican, but in the middle of his voyage, he gave it a new name based on the coat of arms of his sponsor—the guy who put up all the money for the trip. And when a female deer appears on a coat of arms, it's called a hind. Hence the Golden Hind."

"C'mon, tell me the truth. You didn't just happen to know that because you read a lot of history books."

Chance laughed. "Okay, the first time I came here, I wondered the same as you. I did an internet search and in five minutes had all the information."

"Now for the harder question," I said as we pulled

into a parking space. "Why would a restaurant that's over a hundred miles from the ocean be named after a ship?"

"That one's easy. Because the owner of the restaurant was in the navy, and his passionate hobby is sailing."

"You didn't learn that from the internet."

"No, I learned that from the hostess who seated me. Remember, that's what I do—ask questions. Sometimes you can get the answer from a machine, but other times you can't get away from talking to flesh and blood people."

"Speaking of flesh and blood people, I suppose you're wondering why I asked you to come to lunch today with my parents."

Chance smiled. "I did think it was a little soon to be meeting the parents. Strictly speaking, we haven't even been out on a date yet. Things seemed to be moving along a little fast."

"Yeah, well, don't get the wrong idea. I'm not trying to rush you into anything, and I'm not planning to be rushed. It's just that this is the first time I've been together with both my parents since I was twelve years old and thought it would be nice to have someone along who is definitely on my side."

Chance squeezed my arm. "I'm always on your side," he said seriously.

"You saved me from a murder charge; I know whose side you're on."

"When you filled me in on the way over about how your parents have been apart for years and now are deciding to try getting back together again, I'll admit that it sounded strange, but kind of wonderful as well. I believe marriages are intended to last, and this one has even survived betrayal and divorce."

"Let's not get too misty eyed just yet. We'll have to see how things work out. I doubt that either one of them has stopped being a complex and difficult person. And I've been so angry at my mother for so long that I'm not sure I can accept her back after just one luncheon."

"From what you've told me, you've got a lot to forgive your father for as well."

"That's true, too."

Chance looked out across the parking lot. "You remember that passage I found in the Bible when I used it as a way to get a lead in your case?"

"Something about a mother and an ungrateful child, wasn't it?"

"It was a verse from Proverbs. 'A wise son maketh a glad father: but a foolish man despiseth his mother.' Since there were no mothers that I knew about involved in the case, I couldn't figure out how the passage was relevant."

"Well, Maggie was like a mother to everyone, and Travis treated her badly."

"You see, it was a good hint, but I wasn't smart enough to interpret it. But now I think that it applies to your situation as well. I'm sure your father is very proud of you, but you also need a mother's love. It would be foolish of you not to recognize that. I'm sure with some prayer, you'll find a way to forgive her."

"You had me until the word 'prayer.' But I'll certainly give what you're saying some thought."

Chance nodded. "Maybe some day the word 'prayer' won't frighten you so much."

"I'm not frightened. I'm just not convinced."

"Follow your heart and your mind will come along."

Normally I would have made a sharp retort to that. But I realized that, in a way, my love for Chance was a gamble that was dragging my mind along kicking and screaming.

"What's going to happen to Maggie?" I asked.

"She's got a good lawyer."

"Thanks to you."

"And I'm sure he'll make much of Maggie's stressed state of mind when she committed the murder. She'll end up doing some prison time, but how long will depend on the judge and jury."

"I hope it's not very long. You know, I keep thinking how it was the kind of thing that almost anyone could have done under the circumstances."

"That's the thing about bad actions. Most of us are capable of doing them given the right provocation."

"I've been wondering a lot about that lately. I've come to the conclusion that I should be more forgiving. If I can forgive Maggie for murdering someone, I should be able to forgive almost anyone for anything. So I guess you're right, and I should try hard to forgive my mother. I think I'll start by inviting her to go out for a cup of coffee with me a few times—nothing intense, just a chance for us to get to know each other. After all, we are almost strangers."

"That sounds like a fine way to start." Chance checked his watch. "Why don't we go in the restaurant? Your folks might be here already."

I looked at my watch. "It's only just time. My father never shows up on time. It's part of his absent-minded professor act. He's chronically unpunctual, always at least ten minutes late."

"But I'm not," Chance said firmly. "I believe in being punctual."

Perhaps I'd latched onto a man who would prove nearly as difficult as my father. But I was up to the challenge.

Inside, the restaurant was designed as a country inn. When we went through the front door, a young woman serving as hostess took us across a large room.

"Is there anything you'd like to ask her?" I whispered to Chance.

He smiled and shook his head.

On the walls were pictures of grand sailing vessels, and the floor was constructed of wide, highly polished planks that echoed like the deck of an old ship. Although the room was crowded with diners, we were fortunate to get a table by a large window that looked out across the nicely landscaped back lawn to the trees beyond.

When we were seated, I smiled at Chance and said, "Remember, this is my treat. I'm celebrating the return of my mother and getting out of a close scrape."

"I've already been well paid by the station, but I will graciously accept your gift. Will your father be as gracious?"

"He'll have to be. From now on we're playing by new rules."

"Does he know them?"

I grinned. "I'm making them up as we go along."

"I can tell you've been doing a lot of thinking about things."

I nodded. "Lately I've been thinking more about

what I want my life to be like. Although I enjoy meteorology and feel that it does provide a public service, I want to do more for my community. So I've volunteered to go into a middle school and work with students having trouble in math."

"You as a teacher." Chance gave a dry laugh.

"What's so funny?"

"I'm not sure I see you having the patience."

"I'll work at it," I snapped.

"Well, I'm sure that teaching will please your father."

"I suppose it will, but I'm doing it for me. And I've also been thinking that there's another way in which I should be more understanding."

"How's that?"

I reached over and took his hand.

"You know I like you a great deal, but my father has always warned me to avoid handsome, charming men. My experience with Rick certainly proved him right. But now I've decided that you can't follow general rules when it comes to people. You have to judge the specific individuals. And there is nothing shallow or unreliable about you. You stand firm for what you believe…like a rock. That's the kind of man I want."

Chance squeezed my hand, and a teasing smile came over his face. "Would this newfound openness extend to attending church with me on Sunday?"

I frowned. "Why not? But remember, I'll be there as a critic and making up my own mind."

"I'm sure you will."

I glanced across the room.

"Oh, here come my parents now."

Chance made to release my hand, but I held firm.

"They may as well get used to my hanging onto you now because they're going to see a lot more of it in the future."

A word about the author...

Glen Ebisch taught philosophy in college for over twenty-five years, and for the same period of time has been writing mysteries, first for young people, then for adults. He has been fortunate enough to have over twenty published. He lives with his wife in western Massachusetts and now focuses full time on writing, exercise, and travel.

http://www.glenebisch.com